One Morning
In May

This book is dedicated to Ruth,
my sister-in-law who gave me inspiration!

One Morning In May

Patrick B Hayes

Photographs by Michael Madden

Drawings by Mandy Farrar

BREWIN BOOKS

Published by Brewin Books Ltd
Studley, Warwickshire B80 7LG in 2002
www.brewinbooks.com

www.maryashford.co.uk

ISBN 1 85858 193 1

British Library Cataloguing in Publication Data
A Catalogue record for this book is available from the British Library.

Typeset and Printed by SupaPrint (Redditch) Limited,
Unit 19, Enfield Industrial Estate, Redditch, Worcs, B97 6BZ.
www.supaprint.com

ACKNOWLEDGEMENTS

Many thanks to: Awards for All, Robert Pritchard, Kevin Duffey, John Smallwood and all members of the Mary Ashford Society. Chris Ryan, John Wellington, (Mail On Sunday) Peter and Sylvia Chatland, Estepona, Spain, Pilar de la Pena, Oviedo, Spain, Pilar and Miguel, Madrid, Spain. Department of Leisure and Culture Birmingham City Council, Pat Spencer, Clare Hayes, Sally Potter, Bernie Woulf, Zarina Sangra, P. Bowles, Birmingham Public Libraries and all those who have helped with publication.

Prologue

The mystery you are about to read has baffled historians, writers, amateur sleuths, and many others that have engaged in this true story for nearly two hundred years now. In this version of the story I have created a fictional character, a Reverend Martin Finnarty, who is a vicar in the Church of England. Father Martin not only recalls the historical facts but lets the characters from that time tell the story, the mystery, in order to give a true sense of time and place.

Father Martin in his study

Chapter One. St Winifred's Vicarage, Lower Stretton, Worcestershire.

Present Day.

My name is Martin Finnarty and I am the vicar of St Winifred's at Lower Stretton, Worcestershire. It's a pleasant place but I do have my work cut out as I have several smaller parishes to cover so I'm kept quite busy.

St Winifred's Vicarage is an old Victorian Vicarage and I have been here for some time now. I spend quite a lot of my time in the study and I suppose it's become part of me. It contains my favourite books, such as "Butler's Lives of the Saints" St Theresa's, "Interior Castle," and the "History of English Parish Churches."

As well as the usual "Tools of the trade" a cassock, surplice and various liturgical necessaries, I also keep my prized possession, a cricket bat, in the corner. I still turn out for the Clergy X1 and was top scorer last season - 100 not out against the Methodists!

I know a lot of people, especially if they don't attend church, think vicars are eccentrics who are oblivious to reality. I don't consider myself eccentric. The only thing that may be considered eccentric about me is that I insist on having "England's Glory" matches when lighting my pipe. I never buy anything else. If I were asked why I probably wouldn't know except that I like the picture of the steamship on the front of the box. It reminds me of all the places that I never went to but could imagine going to.

I have a cat called Chivers. He is named after the honey and the famous Tottenham Hotspur centre forward, Martin Chivers.

It was quite odd how I became involved in this extraordinary mystery. It was last year in late September and some friends of mine had invited me to spend a weekend in Birmingham. I have always liked Birmingham and have fond memories of my time there. I was a student in the early seventies: I studied theology at Birmingham University.

We had been at the theatre on the Saturday evening and had seen an excellent production of, "The Tempest." Later that night, as we were having a nightcap by the fire and discussing the production we had just seen, my friend's daughter, Zara, arrived home. I can't recall the exact reason, but as we all sat in the soft light by the open fire, Zara told us this strange tale. I suppose the best way to describe it, is a "Murder mystery." Although tired, I was captivated by Zara's words and I listened attentively as she brought the past back to life.

I slept soundly that night but the next day as I drove back to Lower Stretton; Zara's words kept coming back to me. They stayed with me until I went to bed that night and even then as I slept I could hear an echo of Zara's voice. Names, dates and places spun round my world of sleep. Zara certainly was a good storyteller and like a good play or book, her words were memorable and in this case intriguing.

Over the past year I have been studying the case, which has become more fascinating by the day. Little did I know that Zara's words that night would open so many doors. Doors into the past, doors into the imagination and doors into a world we know little of.

The story began almost two hundred years ago in a Warwickshire village that long ago was swallowed up by the huge industrial city of Birmingham. Those that lived then may be gone and their names footnotes in history. However, that night in Birmingham Zara breathed life once more into the very hearts of those that lived and turned back the pages of the past. Those hearts do beat again and the stage is set for our first protagonist who was part of the mystery.

His name is George Jackson and he comes from Birmingham. The year is 1817.

Chapter Two. The Village of Erdington, 1817.

I work in the parish of Sutton Coldfield. I work on the roads. I think I shall always remember that morning.

It were a quiet May morning. The dew was still fresh on the grass and there was a slight mist over the fields. It was still hanging over them when I was nearing my workplace by Webster's wire factory on Penns Mill Lane. A long day loomed in front of me as I plodded along the lane. It was about five in the morning and when my Martha woke me this morning I didn't want to get up. I live in Hurst Street in Birmingham and last night being Whit Monday we had all gone to the "Bull" to celebrate. I think my head was a bit worse for wear to tell the truth.

I walked from Birmingham to Sutton Coldfield as I do every working day. It's about five- mile on the Turnpike road. I leave the turnpike near the lane by the workhouse and walk along the lane until I come to a track. I take the track as far as the fields and then I walk over the fields beyond Penns Mill to Newhall Fields where I work.

This particular morning, I walked across a harrowed field and climbed over a stile to the field that borders Penns Lane. I remember something catching my eye. I walked to the marl pit. It's no longer used now and is half full of water. I walked up the slope to the pit. There were boot prints but a bit smudged as if whoever had been up there had been struggling with a heavy weight. Then there it was. All lined up in a row - a pair of women's boots and a bundle. I just stared at them not knowing what to do. After a while I picked up a boot, one of them half boots that women wear and noticed there was blood on it. I feared the worst. I made my way to Mr Webster's house, the Hall, Penns Hall but stopped at the first house that I came to. I can't rightly remember as it all happened so quickly. The next thing I knew I was running back to the Marl pit with Lavell. We went back to the pit and I told Lavell to stand over the bundle and shoes to make sure no one meddled with them. I then went back to fetch more help.

As I came away from the footpath and into the field along the lane, I saw some liquid on the grass. I leant down and put my fingers in it and then held my hand up to my face. It was blood. People have said that I said that it was "A lake of blood." I don't know if I said that or not but there was a lot of blood on the grass. I noticed there were drops of blood as if some one had cut themselves and walked off in a hurry. It was about thirty yards from the pit and it was a couple of yards long, shaped in the shape of a triangle.

I came back with a man called Bird, and a man called James Simmonds, two workers on the estate. After looking at the pit James Simmonds went away and came back with a heel rake and a pair of reins. Lavell and Bird started to drag the pit with the rake. I don't know why but I didn't want to stay so I left and made my way to work.

Later that day I came across Lavell and he told me what had happened. The first time they tried with the rake and reins but nothing came up but a load of weed. They tried again, nothing. But on the third attempt Lavell cried, "Got something lads, give me a hand." They rushed to help and then after a few tugs they saw her. It was a body of a woman. They dragged her up the side of the pit. She was all muddied and dripping wet. She was face down and when they turned her over Lavell told me they noticed how pretty she was. There was mud on her face and wet leaves in her hair. Bird tried to clean her up as best he could. When Lavell had finished telling me I just stared at the ground for a moment. I just thought, pity her poor family.

By this time others had come running over from the hall and factory. No one was quite sure what to do. The master, Mr Webster, was away. Some one said go and fetch Dr Freer. What was the point of calling for Doctor Freer if the poor girl was dead? Because of all the water the body was heavy. Lavell and Bird came back with a door. They put the poor girl's body on it and took her over the field to Lavell's house. Lavell told me that quite a crowd had gathered by now. Some one said that they should get duck boards to protect the evidence. Just as they were bringing the boards it began to rain, just a shower but enough to make where we were all muddy. Also there were so many people wanting to have a look at the pit there were more feet shuffling around than at a dance at Harvest time. As to who left those footprints it could have been the Man in the Moon, so Lavell said.

Lavell also told me that he went into the harrowed field and he noticed that he came across footprints. There was dew on the ground so he could make them out clearly. First of all there were a man's footprints and then there were footprints of a woman.

Looked like the man was after the woman as there was a chase, so Lavell said, the man running after the woman. Then suddenly they came to a stop. He looked down and in the grass it looked like as if some one had been sleeping on it like cows do in the rain. He looked a little closer at the crushed grass and there was an imprint of a body as if some one had lain there.

Dr Freer had been sent for. The sun was up now and it was a beautiful May day. It seemed strange in a way to think it was such a nice day and inside Lavell's house there lay the body of some poor girl. We didn't even know her name.

The next day on my way back from work I called in at Lavell's. I knocked at the door and Fanny Lavell came out, William Lavell's wife. Mary Smith followed shortly after. Fanny told me that Mr Webster, the owner of Penns, had given her the bundle to examine, as well as the bonnet and shoes that I had seen at the top of the pit. Fanny had to deal with the poor creature. She told me that she had to tear most of the clothes off as they were in such a bad state. The girl's gown was very much stained behind and was very dirty with blood and dirt. She held her hand up in front of me and said that the shift the girl had been wearing had a rent up it as long as her hand. Mary then said that on each arm just below the elbow there was a black mark, which appeared to be made by the grasp of fingers.

I couldn't believe it when they said that the poor girl had been murdered. Murdered? Round here? But nothing happens round here. Dr Freer didn't get to Lavell's until 7.30 in the evening. It was too dark to examine the body so he waited until early next morning. The girl's shift had been torn in "An act of violence" so Dr Freer said. Then there was the blood; loads of it round her private parts and thighs. Fanny said that Dr Freer, and he is well respected, scratched his head as how the poor girl had died. The girl must have drowned in the pit he told Fanny and Mary.

There was the torn shift, blood around her private parts and the two small bruises on the girl's arms, halfway between her shoulders and elbows. It was obvious to me she had been pinned down by who ever did it. Fanny then said the dress looked strange, as there were all creases in it. She noticed this before she undressed the poor creature. When she told Dr Freer he scolded her saying what did she expect the poor thing had lain in the water all night. But she told me she protested despite the Doctor being a doctor and all. She said she had to speak up. Dr Freer looked at the dress and was quite astounded, that was the word he used. It could clearly be made out. It was the impression of a man lying on top of her!

Mary Ashford.

I said to Fanny and Mary, "Dr Freer may not be able to help her in this life but he could see to it that the poor thing get justice." They nodded and agreed with me. One thing we all know then is that the poor girl didn't die by accident. I was hoping that all them footprints were just a bit of horseplay -young things like to fool around especially after a dance - and that the poor thing had just fallen in the pit in the dark like. But this was different. I said to Mary and Fanny, "Does anyone know who she is?"

"Yes, " Fanny replied. "She's Mary Ashford and she comes from Erdington."

"Well I never." I said.

Chapter Three. St Winifred's Vicarage.

"She's Mary Ashford and she comes from Erdington." The names Mary Ashford and Erdington were to stay with me and become part of me as I studied the mystery.

I can understand George's re-action. The poor girl was only twenty years of age. She was born in Erdington, November 1796. No one knows the exact date but we do know that she was baptized on New Year's Eve of that year at Aston Parish Church when she was six weeks old. So working backwards, Mary's birthday would have been the 18th or 19th of November.

Her parents lived in a cottage by the Cross Keys public house. She worked as a market gardener and apparently was a barmaid at the Swan in Erdington. Sadly, this endearing, cosy Georgian hostelry was demolished in the early 1960's and was replaced by a windowless, dull, dreadful, red bricked block, which stands to this day as an outstanding monument dedicated to the lack of imagination initiated by town and country planners everywhere! However, I digress. By the time Mary was twenty she wasn't living at home any longer, probably because there were seven other children in the tiny cottage. Mary lived with her Uncle, Mr Coleman, at Langley Heath, which is on the outskirts of Sutton Coldfield. Apparently, his farmhouse still stands there to this day. They obviously had better town and country planners in Langley and were not as keen on demolition as the planners of Erdington. She also used to stay with her Grandfather, who lived on the corner of Bell Lane and the London and Chester Road. Bell Lane is now called Orphanage Road and goes from the High Street to Penns Lane, where Mary's body was found.

By all accounts she was very pretty, being described as the Belle of the Parish. But her life was taken away from her and consequently she never had a sweet heart, marriage, a family, she never even celebrated her 21st birthday. However, we need to know the events that led up to that fateful night. I think the best person to help us is Hannah Cox, Mary's best friend. Hannah lived on Erdington High Street in a cottage just opposite the "Swan." She was a servant in the Machin household and lived with her mother. As to what happened that night I think it is better if Hannah tells the story.

Chapter Four. Hannah Cox's cottage, Erdington. May 1817.

My name is Hannah Cox and I live in the village of Erdington. Well, it's not really a village as there isn't even a church. If you want the church you have to go to Aston down on the road that goes into Birmingham. So, I should say I live in a hamlet! I live with my mother. She re-married after the death of my father and she's now Mrs Butler. We live opposite the Swan, where Mary used to work. I remember the morning of May 26th. How could I ever forget?

It was about ten o'clock in the morning when she came to see me. I work as a servant at Mr Machin's and Mary called there. I opened the door and she stood there with a lovely smile on her face. She was so excited about going to the dance. She had on a pink cotton frock, a straw bonnet and straw coloured ribbons, black stockings, and half boots. She had a clean frock, a white spencer, and a pair of white stockings in a bundle, which she left at my mother's for putting on for the dance that night. We always have a dance at Whitsun and this year it was at the Tyburn House, Daniel Clarke is the landlord and he keeps a fine house. It's on the turnpike road and was called The Three Tuns many years ago. Don't ask me why they changed the name but for some reason the Tyburn House is the Tyburn House and not the Three Tuns. The Friendly Society put on the dance. It's a good idea as the money made provides for many a widow and orphan and there's been enough of them with the war ending only two years ago.

Well, Mary came in all excited. She was a bit out of breath as she had run almost all the way from her Uncle's, Mr Coleman. It was a warm morning for May and she had a basket of fruit and vegetables she was taking to the Birmingham market, which is always on a Monday. She left me her new dress she was going to wear and her spencer as well, and she must have reminded me a hundred times about collecting her dancing shoes from the cobblers. She did go on. She couldn't' wait to show me the dress. She held it up. Bright yellow it was. She looked beautiful.

"Come on Mary," I said, "We better get on, work won't do itself."

She walked off down the High Street. She turned and called back, "Hannah" she shouted.

"What?" I replied.

"You won't forget the shoes will you?"

Before I could reply she walked quickly off laughing to herself.

That evening about six o'clock Mary came back. She said that she had sold all the fruit at Curzon Street bought a bag of sugar to take home and although tired, enjoyed the walk home. She walked with one of our neighbours, a young girl called Anne Hanson, who lives on Woodlands farm near the Hall, Pipe Hayes Hall, the home of Squire Bagot and her Ladyship. She told the girl about the dance and she got all excited and said she would ask her parents is she could go. I could just see the pair of them walking down the road, Mary making the poor young thing excited about the dance and what dresses they would wear. Anyone would think she was going to a fancy Ball at one of the big houses, not a night at the Tyburn!

I asked her if she would like something to eat, but she said no as she were in a hurry to get changed and go to the dance. To be honest so was I. I remember when we came out. It was about half past seven. I looked up to the sky and noticed how red it looked. Blood red.

I said to Mary, "Red sky at night, shepherd's delight!"

Then we walked on to the Tyburn. It was a warm night and the fields were deserted. Now and then you could hear a corncrake but that was all. It were a bit different by the time we got to the Tyburn. You'd think all of England was there. Outside old men sat on stools smoking their pipes and all of the young bucks of the village and beyond stood with their pots of ale, smiling and laughing and slapping each other on the back. We could hear the music upstairs as that's where the dance was. We went up. I acknowledged those I knew on the way. I noticed the lads looking at Mary. Couldn't blame them. It's not a sin to look is it? The dance was in full flow when we got in. The fiddlers were playing away and the boys were swirling the girls around, there was much tobacco smoke and men with pots of beer bumped into us everywhere we went. Mary and I sat down. Within a few seconds I heard a voice say, "Would Madam care to dance?" I looked up expecting to see some gentleman, but it was my intended Ben Carter. I say intended, but I've told him if I have to wait much longer he won't be my intended for much longer. He's promised me I'll always be his sweetheart and he told me only last Easter that as sure as God made apples green we'll be wed before Michaelmas, or thereabouts, so he said.

Well, the night passed well. We had supper. Mary ate little. I scolded her, saying she should eat, but she was thinking more of the dancing and off she went again. When I was at table with Ben I saw Mary dancing with this man. He weren't tall but he was stocky and strong.

"Who's that dancing with Mary?" I said to Ben.

"I don't know," Ben replied. "Never seen him before." And he gulped down more ale.

Well after the dance Mary and him came over to us all smiling and out of breath. He told us that his name was Abraham Thornton and that he came from Castle Bromwich, a mile or so east on the turnpike road. He told us he was a bricklayer and lived with his father, who was a farmer on the Earl of Bradford's estate. He seemed pleasant enough. And you couldn't stop them dancing; they danced as if it was going out of fashion.

Around midnight I thought it best we went home. It had been a long day and

Mary Ashford and Abraham Thornton. Did Fate throw them together that night?

7

Mary had to be at Tamworth market in the morning with her uncle, Mr Coleman. It was hard to persuade her to leave the floor. I know she was enjoying herself but I thought she had had enough time dancing with Mr Thornton. I told her that Ben and me would meet her on the canal bridge outside.

We waited on the bridge for about a quarter of an hour and Mary still hadn't come out. So I sent Ben back in for her. Ben came back out and said that Thornton was dancing with Mary but she said she was coming. We waited about a quarter of an hour and eventually Mary and Abraham came out. I said to Abraham,

"Well it has been a pleasure meeting you Mr Thornton and we'll bid you goodnight. Mary has to rise early tomorrow."

"What, and have you ladies walk home alone." He said almost shouting.

"Benjamin is with us." I told him as I knew what he was wanting.

"Surely Ben you can't walk Hannah to Erdington and Mary to Langley Heath?" Ben was about to speak when Mary replied.

"There is no need. Why don't we all walk together as far as the lane on the

Abraham notices Mary enter the dance

turnpike? Ben can walk with you Hannah, and Mr Thornton can escort me to my Grandfather's. It's only up a bit from the lane and I can stay there the night. He won't mind."

"And what about your work clothes? You'll need them for market?"

"I'll come in the morning, Hannah."

I agreed to what she said but to be honest I wasn't too happy about it all. We had walked a little way when I noticed that I had left my bracelet in the Tyburn. I told Ben to go back and get it. As I waited Mary and Abraham slowly drifted off. I thought no harm would come of it. Ben came back with my bracelet about half way between Mrs Reeves's house and old man Potter's place. It was a moonlit night so the road was clear. A slight breeze blew. I put my arm through Ben's and we walked as far as Grange Lane. I said goodnight to Ben and he walked with Abraham and Mary to the next turning. When I got home mother was asleep as I could hear her snoring. I could hear the clock strike and it was no more than one o'clock.

I was only asleep for a while when I heard a knocking at the door. I lit a candle

Abraham, Mary, Ben and Hannah leaving the Tyburn

and gathered up my nightdress and came downstairs. I was a little scared, as I didn't know who it was. When you get a knock at the door in the middle of the night, you fear the worst. Many years ago an Innkeeper at the Roebuck heard shouting in the street, opened the window to see what all the commotion was about and he were shot dead. To this day no one knows who did it. Well, when you hear a commotion you have to be careful. Anyway I was worried about my mother being woken.

I opened the door and there stood Mary. "Mary" I exclaimed, "Where have you been to this hour?"

She told me that she had stayed at her grandfather's on Bell Lane. When I asked her about Mr Thornton she said that she had been with him for a good bit. I asked her where he was and she said that he had gone home. I lit another candle so she could change her clothes. She stood up all the time while she was changing and

Mary makes her way home. A home she never reached.

didn't sit down. I asked her where she was going and she said that she was going to her grandfather's again. We talked for about twenty minutes and as I told his Worship at the court she looked in fine spirits and not at all troubled. She changed her clothes but I remember she kept her dancing shoes on and put her ordinary shoes in the bundle she took with her. Why, I don't know. Maybe she forgot.

I had only closed the door a second when she tapped on the door again. I opened the door and let her in. She had forgotten the sugar she had bought in Birmingham. She picked up the sugar and off she went. I never saw her again.

Chapter Five. St Winifred's Vicarage.

Mary may have been comely, young and desirable but she was not perfect. For a reason known only to herself she lied to Hannah. She said she had stayed at her Grandfather's when she clearly hadn't and instead of being with Abraham, "for a good bit" had indeed been with him from just after midnight to knocking on Hannah's cottage door, nearly four hours. None of us is perfect. We all lie and are economical with the truth. So did Mary, she wanted to protect herself and probably didn't want a lengthy discussion about her time with Abraham.

So what do we know as fact? They left the Tyburn House after midnight and walked up the Turnpike road, the London and Chester Road. Then it seems they turned left at Bell lane that leads to Penns Mills Lane, as it was called then, not far from where Mary's body was found.

A man named John Humpage was visiting the house of Mr Reynolds, at Penns as he was courting his daughter. As Humpage sat inside the house he heard voices in the lane outside. The talking continued until Humpage decided to go home to Witton in Aston. He walked across a footpath that led to a foredrough, which is a kind of track that leads through a field, and then onto Bell Lane. As he approached the foredrough he saw two people sitting on a stile. He immediately recognized Abraham Thornton as he knew him. He bade him good morning and Thornton returned the greeting. The girl, however, he did not recognize as she held her head down so he could not see who it was. Did Mary know Humpage and if so was she ashamed to be seen with Thornton after being with him for three hours? When Humpage saw them it was about three o'clock in the morning. He left them sitting against the stile and walked home to Witton.

The next fact we know is that Mary was seen walking hastily down Bell Lane, about five minutes away from Erdington and Mrs Butler's house, where Hannah resided. The time was now half past three and a Thomas Asprey, a resident of Erdington, saw her. She came to Hannah's at about four o'clock, changed her clothes and after about fifteen minutes left to make her way back to Sutton Coldfield.

As she left Hannah's, a waggoner, John Kesterton, delivering milk saw her. He remembers seeing her and he knew it was Mary and he cracked his whip to get her attention. Mary was then seen walking back down Bell Lane towards Sutton Coldfield by a workman called Joseph Dawson. She was walking very fast and as we know was now wearing her working clothes which included a scarlet spencer. The one she had worn at the dance was white. A man called Thomas Broadhurst saw her again near the foredrough and she was still walking very fast. This was the last person who saw Mary alive. When Broadhurst got home he looked at his clock and determined that the time was twenty-five minutes past four o'clock. It was around six o'clock that our friend George Jackson discovered, what was later known as "A lake of blood." Somewhat dramatic maybe but there was sufficient blood for George to be concerned. He followed the trail of blood in that eventually led to the fatal field as it became known, where he saw the shoes and bundle lying close to the marl pit.

When a body has been discovered the normal practice is to call the police. However, in 1817 there was no police force in Erdington. The nearest arm of the law lay in Birmingham. However, rural communities act quickly in these circumstances and Daniel Clarke, the Landlord of the Tyburn, was swiftly sworn in as special constable. It was his task to find Thornton, arrest him and make him give an account of his actions the previous evening. No one knows for sure who told Clarke that they knew that Thornton was the last person to be seen with Mary. It may have been Hannah or it may have been John Humpage, but whatever, Clarke was dispatched to find Thornton, who had become the main suspect. So once more into the past, dear friends!

Chapter Six. Daniel Clarke, Innkeeper. The Tyburn House, Erdington. 1817.

There came a knocking on my door that morning. I was busy clearing up from the dance we had the night before. It had finished late and as with all good dances there was a lot of clearing up to be done. The last one that said, "Goodnight Daniel" said so as the sun was coming up! I can put money on a few aching heads this morning.

It came as a shock to me when they said that Mary had lost her life and had been violated and thrown into a pit. I remember her dancing till midnight. I know her and knew her as a lovely lass.

I saddled my horse and took the road to Castle Bromwich. I came to the church by castle hill when I saw him, Thornton that is, riding on a pony. I said to him,

"What became of the young woman that went away with you from my house last night?"

He just sat on his pony and stared at me, making no reply.

I said, "She is murdered!"

"Murdered?" he said.

"Yes, murdered and thrown into a pit."

"Why," he replied, "I was with her till four o'clock this morning."

"Then," said I, "You must come along with me and clear yourself."

He said. "I can soon do that."

Tyburn House 1817

We rode back to the Tyburn, which is only a mile away from the chapel. I thought it strange, as he never talked about how the poor girl met her fate. Instead he wanted to talk to me only about farming, which I thought was a curious thing. He had danced with her until midnight and then walked with her to four but not a word did he utter about her. I don't know if he was ashamed or trying to hide his guilt but he insisted on talking about pleasantries. I thought he must either be a heartless rogue or a simpleton!

I took him back to the Tyburn. He put his pony in the stable and he said that he wanted to walk over the grounds, the footway to Sutton, which I thought was a bit strange. We both went inside and I gave him something to eat and drink. He seemed more composed and we waited for the constable to come from Birmingham. The constable, Constable Dale arrived about ten o'clock and Thornton was taken into custody. Dale took him upstairs and ordered him to take off his coat, in order to inspect his clothing, which he did. When I came into the room I saw Dale holding Thornton's shirt and I noticed that the bottom of the shirt was blood stained. Now I know in this good country of ours a man is innocent until proved guilty but with blood on his shirt and blood in the field and Mary now dead, I couldn't help but think Thornton had a hand in this terrible business.

13

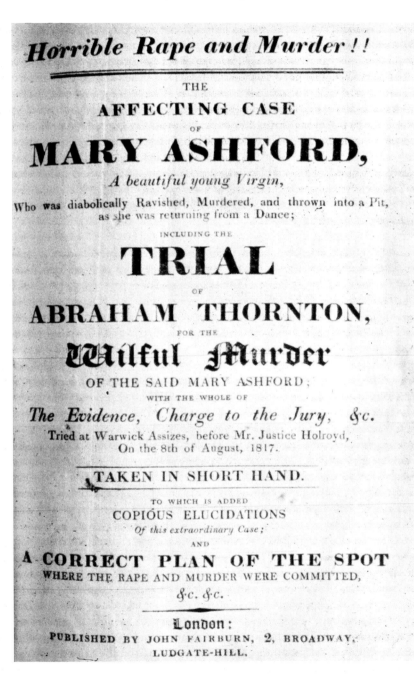

Horrible Rape and Murder !!

THE
AFFECTING CASE
OF
MARY ASHFORD,
A beautiful young Virgin,

Who was diabolically Ravished, Murdered, and thrown into a Pit,
as she was returning from a Dance;

INCLUDING THE

TRIAL
OF
ABRAHAM THORNTON,
FOR THE

Wilful Murder

OF THE SAID MARY ASHFORD;
WITH THE WHOLE OF

The Evidence, Charge to the Jury, &c.
Tried at Warwick Assizes, before Mr. Justice Holroyd,
On the 8th of August, 1817.

TAKEN IN SHORT HAND.

TO WHICH IS ADDED
COPIOUS ELUCIDATIONS
Of this extraordinary Case;
AND

A CORRECT PLAN OF THE SPOT
WHERE THE RAPE AND MURDER WERE COMMITTED,

&c. &c.

London:
PUBLISHED BY JOHN FAIRBURN, 2, BROADWAY,
LUDGATE-HILL.

Front page of the record of Thornton's Trial.

14

At one o'clock Mr Bedford, who lives at Birches Green in Erdington, came. He is the Magistrate and Thornton gave him what's called a deposition, which means he told Mr Bedford what happened that night in his own words. He said that he met Mary at the dance and they had walked off together. He said that they had come to a stile and then walked over four or five fields. They then walked back to the stile where a man wished them good morning. He then walked with Mary to Mrs Butler's house in Erdington. They stopped at the green and then Mary walked on by herself. He waited some time for her to return but as she didn't come back, he went towards home.

He admitted to Mr Bedford that he had a connection with her but that she was as willing as he was, but as for murder, he denied it quite plainly.

Chapter Seven. St Winifred's Vicarage.

Oh dear, it's not looking too clever for Mr Thornton, is it? He admitted having intercourse with the girl. He had to say it was with consent as rape was a capital offence as well as murder. Near the scene of the crime boot prints were found running across open fields, past Pype Hayes Hall until they stopped by the Turnpike Road. On inspecting the boot prints it was soon discovered that one of the boots had a nail missing from it Thornton had a nail missing from one of his boots. Another bootmark was discovered at the top of the pit but it was hard to distinguish if it had a nail missing or not. However, the print was quite deep in the ground and had moved about rather as though the person had thrown a heavy weight. In this case it was determined that the heavy weight was the body of Mary! This evidence, with the admittance of intercourse and blood on his shirt was enough CIRCUMSTANTIAL evidence, if not to convict, certainly to bring the accused to trial. To be fair there could have been any number of men's boots with a nail missing, but it does seem quite coincidental doesn't it? Also, if Mary lied, then so did Thornton. He said that he walked Mary back to Erdington and waited on the village green, yet more than one witness said they saw Mary walk back to Hannah's ALONE! If Thornton wasn't lying then the witnesses were either mistaken or for some unknown reason wittingly perjured themselves in a court of law. If we discount the witnesses, then Thornton's account rings true. Both had been drinking, both were in the flush of youth and what may have started out as a bit of "Canoodling" led to something much more passionate. Mary may have been seen as the Belle of the Parish but she was young, and above all, human. We can all be victims of temptation, how many times have I seen Chivers gazing with delight into my fishpond! Maybe Thornton had promised her marriage and seduced her into giving up her virginity. Oh yes, she had been a virgin up to the point of submitting herself. Dr Freer who examined the body said she had been a virgin until connection took place that is why there was blood around her genitals as her hymen had been broken. Dr Freer stated in his own words,

"Between the thighs and the lower parts of the legs there was a good deal of blood. The parts of generation were lacerated, and a quantity of coagulated blood was about those parts. There were two lacerations of the parts of generation quite fresh. I was perfectly convinced that until those lacerations the deceased was a virgin."

Forensic science was in its infancy in 1817 but Freer was able to determine that this was the case. Also, reading the coroner's report of the day she was suffering from the, "Menses" brought about by the dancing. In other words she was menstruating, as Dr Freer explained,

"The exercise of dancing was likely to have accelerated the menses. There was an unusual quantity of blood.

Now, although many of my parishioners may disagree, I think I am a liberal minded man. However, my imagination has to be stretched to conceive the possibility of a young woman, on having known a man for only a few hours, a virgin, menstruating, would go into a field and have sex with a virtual stranger. Furthermore, she knew the social and moral consequences of such an act, especially in such a small rural community. If Thornton was "Jack the lad" the news of his conquest would soon travel fast and "Comely Mary" would be no more. I am not moralizing, but the social mores of yesterday are so much different from those of today. In Mary's day, it was in living memory that fornicators were tied to a cart and whipped in public!

It has been argued that Mary had been unaware that she was menstruating and that all the blood discovered was because of her period and not because her hymen had been broken. However, Dr Freer said,

"The menses do not produce such blood as that. I had no doubt that the blood in the fields came from the lacerations I saw."

This is a most puzzling case! Why did both protagonists lie when they didn't really have to? Thornton could have said that he had sex with Mary in the field and having got what he wanted, his behaviour being more akin to an alley cat than a respectable human being, wandered off home instead of seeing Mary safely back to Hannah's. Likewise, Mary could have told the truth and said that she was with him all the time instead of telling Hannah that she had been at her Grandfather's house.

It would take a trial to determine the true facts. Thornton was kept in custody in Birmingham until August of that year when he was taken to Warwick Crown Court to be tried for the wilful murder of the one said Mary Ashford.

Chapter Eight. Warwick Assizes. August 1817.

My name is Tobias Howard and I am a reporter with the Birmingham Gazette often known as Aris's Gazette. I was asked to go to Warwick and give a report for our readers on the most heinous crime that was committed in the parish of Sutton Coldfield, May last. I could not help but note that no trial since the year of 1781 when the unfortunate Captain Donellan was convicted of poisoning his brother-in-law, Sir Theodosius Boughton ever so excited all ranks of people. I had travelled from Birmingham to Warwick the night before and had found suitable lodgings. I rose early and when I arrived at the courthouse at six o'clock in the morning a great number of persons had gathered outside, using every interest, endeavour and entreaty to gain admission. The trial was due to commence at eight o'clock and everyone was pressing against the doors. So much so that the Javelin men found it difficult to make a passage for the witnesses and those called to the trial to enter.

The courtroom was crowded to excess. Mr Clarke, Sergeant Copley and Mr Perkins were counsel for the prosecution and Mr Reader and Mr Reynolds for the prisoner. Mr Justice Holroyd oversaw the proceedings. The prisoner, dressed in a long black coat, yellow waistcoat, coloured breeches and stockings emerged into the court room and he was charged with the following,

"On the 27th of May last in the Royal Town, Manor and Lordship of Sutton Coldfield, in the County of Warwick, not having the fear of God before his eyes, but being moved by the instigation of the Devil, wilfully murdered Mary Ashford, by throwing her into a pit of water."

A great silence fell when the accusation was read out.

The prisoner, Thornton, pleaded, "Not guilty" and the trial began with the Judge, Mr Justice Holroyd saying, "God send you a good deliverance."

When the jury was named William Smith was objected to and excluded. The following persons were then sworn in:

George Hues, of Kenilworth, Farmer.
Thomas Pepe, of Kenilworth, Comb-maker.
John Harrison, of Birmingham, Steel-worker.
Isaac Green, of Lapworth, Farmer.
Joseph Johnson, of Knowle, Draper.
John Crooke, of Studley, Needle-maker.
William Bennet, of Bilton, Farmer.
John Alibone, of Bilton, Farmer.
George Tandy, of Hampton-in-Arden, Yeoman.*
John Tibbits, of Hampton-in-Arden, Yeoman.
Thomas Johns, of Lapworth, Farmer.
Joseph Burge, of Lapworth, Farmer.

*George Tandy is sometimes referred to as Clarke Tandy.

The trial lasted all day and many witnesses were called. It turned out to be a most fascinating case. Like so many there that day I did not know of the deceased but she must have been a fine lady indeed. Mr Clarke, (King's Counsel) described her as,

"A young girl of the most fascinating manners, of lovely person, in the bloom and prime of her life and who up to the period of this horrible transaction had borne the most irreproachable character."

I noticed many heads nodding in agreement. I was more than startled as were all those present when the prisoner actually **ADMITTED** having connection with her but with blood being discovered on his shirt when he was taken into custody he had to mitigate the circumstances somehow. It was plausible then, as the connection took place in a field at night, he would not have been aware of the great amount of blood that issued from her onto his clothing.

However, what he could not give account to, were the footprints. Allow me to explain. On entering the harrowed field from the foredrough, footprints of a woman can be clearly made out. The footsteps stop some yards after entering the field. They stop quite abruptly and it became apparent that the reason she stopped was because some one was now standing in front of her blocking her way. Instead of retreating, the girl, determined to get home, tried to run round the person who was impeding her way. A chase then ensued with the footprints first dodging, then walking, then dodging and then running. It would seem obvious that Mary must have been acquainted with her assailant. If she had been gripped by fear then she would have turned tail and run as if her life depended on it, back to Erdington. He couldn't deny that he wasn't in the field that night as there were a multitude of boot prints. Whoever wore those boots had a nail missing from one of them, and, as we know, Thornton had a nail missing from one of his boots.

Although Thornton refused to give an account of himself his lawyers spoke on his behalf. In Thornton's Defence, it was conveyed to the jury and those in the public gallery that the chase was nothing more than, "Horseplay." Mary had willing gone into the field with him. It was a moonlit night so a playful chase which young lovers may want to do would be possible. It was when he caught her that they were engulfed by a powerful passion. A night of dancing, drinking and frolicking on a warm summer's evening is a heady brew, which sadly led to tragedy this particular May night.

However, it seems that one of the Seven Deadly Sins had already entered his heart well before he went into the field with Mary. According to a one John Cooke a farmer of Erdington the all consuming, all cogent sin of **LUST** had sown its seeds in the soul of Thornton as he saw Mary enter the dance room at the Tyburn House. Mr Clarke, prosecuting, examined Cooke. He gave the following evidence.

"I saw the prisoner there that night and I also saw the deceased Mary Ashford come into the room. When Mary Ashford came in I heard the prisoner ask Mr Cottrell who she was, and Cottrell said, 'It's old Ashford's daughter.' I then heard the prisoner say, 'I know a sister of hers, and have been connected with her three times, and I will with her or die for it.' I am quite sure I heard the prisoner say those very words, which were spoken not to me but to Cottrell."

The court was appalled at what Cooke had told them. Cottrell denied that he ever heard the prisoner say what Cooke had stated. I waited for Cottrel to make an

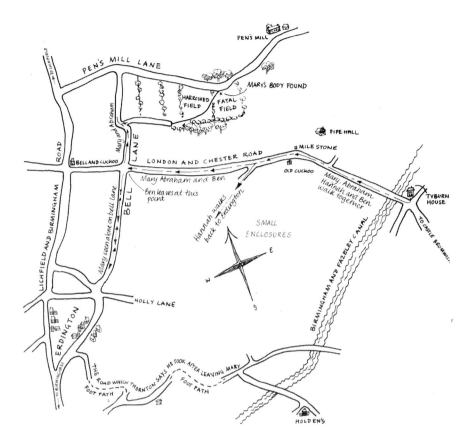

Route taken by Mary, after leaving Tyburn House.

appearance and give an account of what Cooke had told the court. He never was summoned, which I thought most strange, especially as Cooke later said that Cottrell did not deny it in front of him and his associates at a later date!

The jury of twelve honest men, good and true, observed thoughtfully Thornton's account, even if he had not delivered it personally. For the prosecution, his antics in the field that night were seen as more sinister than mere horseplay. So sinister indeed that as the connection took place under a tree, it has become known as the "Violation Tree." The prosecution was also very zealous to hear Thornton's explanation of how during "Horseplay" that her shift became ripped and why there were bruises on her upper arms. It would seem that yes, Mary did give consent to go into the field and that she did take part in some foolishness but she soon was like a fly in a spider's web and the spider had his way with her!

The prosecution said that after the connection took place by force, he panicked,

19

as he knew he had committed a most foul and heinous crime. His heart must have pounded with fear and chills must have run down his spine at the very thought of what the consequences of his actions might be! What words did she utter as she lay ravished in the dew, her arms bruised, her shift torn, her blood seeping like a stream into the grass?

" You have violated me, Abraham Thornton. Violated me! I'll see that you hang for this!"

One paid the ultimate price for connection without consent as one does for taking a fellow person's life. If this be so Thornton may have thought, "Might as well be hanged for stealing a sheep as well as a lamb," and done the poor girl in by throwing her into the pit.

The esteemed members of the Jury passed the day listening to a multitude of testaments. At eight o'clock in the evening they gave their verdict. They didn't even leave the courtroom as they were so assured in the agreement. They found Abraham Thornton **NOT GUILTY** for the wilful murder of the said Mary Ashford.

Penns Lane 1817. The marl pit where Mary was found. (Photo was taken 1901.)

The public gallery was in uproar and I could see quite clearly the distress the verdict caused the members of Mary's family. It was as if they had all been summoned to Hades itself, as the denial of justice was too much of a burden to bear! I know of late the outrage the populace not just of county but of country have come to express in most virulent tones at this tragedy and the deep desire for Justice the good citizens have continually clamoured for. I count myself as one of those seekers of retribution but I also stand by the very worthy laws of this land. Laws that have made this country what it is today. Justice must be done and it was. Mr Thornton was able to vindicate himself and give assurance of his innocence!

Chapter Nine. St Winifred's Vicarage.

Mr Thornton had an alibi all right. Shortly after Mary was attacked and thrown into the pit Thornton was seen two and a half miles away at Castle Bromwich. It's quite complicated so you'll have to pay attention and that includes you, Chivers!

Mary left Hannah's house about four o' clock. She was seen by the waggoner and then by Thomas Broadhurst, who as we know was the last person to see Mary alive. This would have been about four fifteen in the morning. She was nearly at the top of Bell Lane so she was only minutes away from the fatal field. Thornton on the other hand was seen at half past four two and a half miles away by a milkman called William Jennings. Thornton was coming from Erdington towards Castle Bromwich and Jennings described him as,

"Walking very leisurely along the road without the least appearance of heat or hurry about him."

Thornton also had a degree of fortune on his side. Jennings was standing about thirty yards from Holden's farmhouse. The farmhouse is about a hundred yards from the Birmingham and Fazeley canal. Jennings saw Thornton walking towards him, towards the farmhouse from the Canal Bridge. Where Thornton had come from would prove vital in the case. Mr Clarke cross- examined Jennings and asked him,

"Could you tell whether he came down the towing path of the canal or down the lane from Erdington?"

Jennings answered, "No, I can't tell that, I did not see him until he was twenty yards from me."

If Jennings had seen Thornton come **OFF** the tow path then it supported the prosecution's case that he was indeed the murderer in that after murdering Mary he had run across country then on to the towpath near the Tyburn House, finally emerging near Holden's to establish a convenient alibi. If on the other hand he was seen coming down Gig lane, (now known as Holly Lane), which leads to Erdington, Thornton's testimony of seeing Mary home would seem to be a credible explanation.

Jennings's wife, Martha was cross-examined by Sergeant Copley. He asked her, "Where were you standing when you first saw the prisoner?"

"In the road near Mr Holden's house."

"Much nearer the house than the canal bridge?"

"Yes."

"How long had you been in this position?"

"About five minutes. We were looking at a cow that was running at a great rate down the lane; when she had passed us we turned round to look after her, and then we saw the prisoner."

Copley then asked her a pertinent question,

"Then as your backs were towards the prisoner, he might have come along the towing path without you seeing him?"

Martha responded with a simple, "Yes."

Martha was re-examined by Mr Reynolds who was defending Thornton. He established that both William and Jennings had walked **ALONG** the towpath from Birmingham that morning. He asked Martha,

"You walked some distance along the towing path, and you saw nobody coming along it then? Nobody? The prisoner, you say, was walking very leisurely, when he passed you?"

Martha again responded with, "Yes."

Thornton had then walked past Holden's farm. (The site of the farm is where the gatehouse of Fort Dunlop stands). In the farmhouse a young servant girl called Jane Heaton was looking out of her bedroom window when she saw Thornton walk by. Despite being in an elevated position she was unable to tell what direction Thornton had come from. Furthermore, she described Thornton as "Walking quite slowly." It was then between four thirty and twenty to five. When Jane came downstairs she said,

"I saw Jennings and his wife; they came to ask what o'clock it was and I looked at my master's clock to tell them. I t wanted seventeen minutes to five."

The farmer's son John Holden also saw him that morning at the same time. Not only had Thornton established an alibi but also he had successfully confused the prosecution, as they were unable to determine from which direction he had come that night.

Moving swiftly on, Thornton made his way home to Castle Bromwich. He met John Haydon, Mr Rotten's gamekeeper, who was taking up some nets at the floodgates on the river. It was about five in the morning. Mr Woodcock the miller saw the two men chatting and he thought it was about ten past five. We can see then what problems the prosecution had as Thornton's alibi was virtually concrete.

The case for the prosecution was now severely weakened. Nevertheless, they still maintained that Thornton went into the field with Mary but despite amorous advances his ardour was thwarted! He then lay in wait for her to return, as he knew she would and when she arrived he confronted her. She wasn't scared at first, as she knew him, hence the dodging, walking and then the **RUNNING!** After raping her and knowing he had committed a capital offence, he threw her in the pit to drown.

He may have even dragged her into the pit and forced her head under the water thus causing drowning. This however all flounders with the timing. He would have had to lay in wait to surprise her, rape her, throw her into the pit and then run over two miles over open country and pop up at Holden's farm, where he was seen by several witnesses. All the witnesses said that he was walking leisurely and without the least appearance of heat or confusion. It was also said at the trial that Thornton had legs like, "Hovel posts" and would have found it difficult to run over open country in such a short time. Those were the facts and the facts spoke plainly. It was highly doubtful that he could have committed the murder and the jury had no option but to let him go free.

The verdict, however, was seen as unsatisfactory to the people of Erdington, Warwickshire and indeed England and most of all to the Ashford family.

Chapter Ten. The Ashford Cottage, Erdington. 1817.

You could have struck me down dead when I heard Thornton had won his liberty. After what he done to my poor sister. Those men in fancy wigs and gowns blinded everyone with their great words and speeches. He's destroyed our family. There's eight of us children. Well, was, as there's only seven now. I'm Ann and I'm the eldest, followed by William who's two years younger than me, followed by Mary, who was four years younger than me. We were the three out of the eight that were born last century, which makes us seem old, when you say it. They chopped the King's head off in France when I was born or thereabouts. There's six years between Mary and the next one down, so it's like two families in one if you can understand that. The little one John is only two years of age so he could be my son not my brother. Another thing that makes me Mary and William the same is that we were all christened on New Year's Eve! Not on the same New Year's Eve of course but on a New Year's Eve at Aston Parish. You would suppose it might have brought us luck.

Well we were blessed by fortune; we were happy, got through childhood. Many a family round here lost little un's. You just have to ask the sexton or look at the graves in the churchyard and you'll understand what I am saying. We were never going to be anyone fancy in the world, not like those who live at the hall, Squire and his lady wife. We knew our place.

When we were little, Father would tell us stories on winter nights. The one that fascinated Mary the most was the one about a boy who ran away to sea and had all these adventures. She would just sit there and stare into nothing. She could hear the story a hundred times but she listened to it as if it were the first time it was ever told! When we were walking through the fields one-day she said to me,

"You know Ann, one day I'm going to find the sea."

"What do you want to be doing that for?" said I.

"I want to be like the boy who ran away. Do you know how far the sea is from here?"

"I don't rightly know. I know that when the stagecoach passes east down the turnpike road they're heading for the sea."

"I wonder what it's like- the sea, I mean. Sometimes, in the summer, in the evening, I listen to the wind blowing through the corn. That's what the sound of the sea must be like I says to myself."

"Mary, what are you going on about?" She just turned and smiled. That girl, she was always dreaming. Well she can dream all she likes now. But I know some one who won't rest easy and that's Mr Thornton, Earl of Bradford or no Earl of Bradford to help him. Your Father, Thornton, may work on his Lordship's estate but he won't help you. He's an honest man. I don't care what any jury said, honest men, good and true they swallowed a pack of lies. Everyone knows what a scoundrel he is. Do you know what he said at the Tyburn House when Mary walked in? He turned round to another of his ale-supping cronies and said, "I've connected with her sister and I'll connect with her or die by it!" Did you hear that? He said that he had connected with me as if I was a common whore! And he was going to do the same to Mary. Well, he did, but not with her consent. She wouldn't give herself up to a brute like that. That's why he had to force himself upon her and she with the menses too, pins her down like an animal. But he still wasn't satisfied. To hide his crime he had to do away with her by throwing her into a pit. He couldn't even show her a shred of mercy. She could have lived with the shame. I would have taken care of her. He used her then threw her away like an old rag.

Well, Mr Abraham Thornton, you think you're safe, don't you, now that you are at liberty once more? I know you've been in scrapes before. Everyone in the parish knows you have a reputation as a "Ladies' man." "Lady killer" more like! And that your father has got you out of many a scrape. Well, he won't be able to help you now.

People of the parish want to see justice. I know the poor didn't get justice but we have fortune on our side now. My brother William is going to appeal. It's in his rights. Lawyers have told him so. So that means you're going to have to stand before us all again except this time you won't be the slippery fish you were before. This time we'll be right. This time they'll find you guilty of my sister's death and this time, Mr Abraham Thornton, you will hang, and I'd pull the rope myself if I could!

Chapter Eleven. St Winifred's Vicarage.

I think Ann had the right to be furious. Not only had her sister been murdered the perpetrator had escaped justice.

"Double Jeopardy," that was the name of the law that Ann mentioned. Quite curious too, as it was almost a forgotten law and rarely used. In modern terms it would be the same as taking out a private prosecution and William Ashford as the direct male heir of the Ashford family was able to take out an appeal. It was a costly business but a public fund was set up to pay for the legal proceedings. According to the records it cost £100.00 just to have the Appeal brought into force. The £100.00

didn't cover all the other fees and expenses: this was a considerable sum at the beginning of the nineteenth century.

"Double Jeopardy" or "Writ of Appeals" had been used in the previous century. In 1709 at Guilford, Surrey, a man called Christopher Slaughterford was hanged after an Appeal of Murder. Later, in 1729, Martin Cluff hanged at Tyburn, having previously been acquitted on Trial of Indictment. Slaughterford's case was apparently similar to Thornton's as the Appeal was lodged in the name of Henry Young, the brother and heir of the deceased.

Ashford's lawyers must have been quite astute to discover such a law. Of course it cannot be out of anger, frustration or mere pique that an "Appeal to Murder" can be used. There has to be new evidence presented or a case made that the evidence at the first trial was either false or mistaken. In this case it was all to do with Time!

I remember one chilly evening when I was walking across the churchyard I heard the church clock strike six. Nothing unusual in that. When I arrived at the vicarage I switched on the radio for the evening news. I switched on the radio in the kitchen to hear the deep tones of the announcer,

"You're listening to Radio Four and this is the news at six o'clock."

I then took a tin of cat food from the cupboard and began opening it with a tin opener. As usual Chivers purred loudly and rubbed his fur against my legs.

"Yes, yes, it's coming. Remember, Patience is a virtue and dear God do we need it at times!" I said to him.

As I emptied the cat food into Chivers' dish I looked up at the electric green coloured clock on my oven and it read, 5.55. Now the point I am trying to illustrate is that in modern twenty first-century society, with all the technology available to it, I noticed that three time sources were all different. The church clock, the BBC and the electronic clock/timer on my cooker. Therefore, what must it have been like in 1817?

It is vital to go over the times again and see if the Ashford family had cause to obtain a "Writ of Appeal" and that Justice was their main quest and not solely revenge!

On Whit Monday 26th May 1817 Mary and Hannah went to the dance together at the Tyburn House.

12.00. Midnight. Mary leaves Tyburn House with Thornton, Hannah and Benjamin Carter.

2.45. a.m. Mary and Thornton were seen talking at the bottom of the Foredrough beside Bell Lane by **JOHN HUMPAGE.**

3.30.a.m. Mary was seen walking fast from Bell Lane towards Erdington by **THOMAS ASPREY.**

4.00.a.m. Mary was seen coming towards Erdington and Mrs Butler's house by **JOSEPH DAWSON.**

4.05. a.m. Mary changed her clothes at Hannah's. (Mrs Butler's.)

4.15. a.m. Mary seen coming out of Hannah's with bundle and going along Bell

Lane in a hurry by **JOHN KESTERTON.** No one else was seen on the road.

4.18. a.m. Mary was seen crossing the road from Erdington to Penn's Mill Lane by **THOMAS BROADHURST**. This was the last time Mary was seen alive.

4.40.a.m. **WILLIAM JENNINGS, MARTHA JENNINGS** and **JANE HEATON** as well as **JOHN HOLDEN** see Thornton.

5.05.a.m. Thornton was seen by **JOHN HAYDON**, Mr Rotten's gamekeeper, about half a mile from Holden's farm. He talked with Thornton for ten to fifteen minutes before setting off to Castle Bromwich.

5.10.a.m. Thornton was seen talking with John Haydon by **JOHN WOODCOCK**.

5.20.a.m. Thornton was seen passing Wheelwright's Bank by employee **MARTIN WHITE** about half a mile from Twamley's Mill.

6.00.a.m. George Jackson discovers Mary's belongings on top of marl pit. Mary's body is taken from pit.

I have always wondered about the times, as they all seemed so neat and exact. This was England 1817 and at that time there was no uniformity of time. This came later with the arrivals of the railways in the 1840's. Also not everyone had a

Mary leaving Hannah's cottage in the early hours of May 27th.

timepiece, i.e. a pocket watch or clock at home.

Let us look at the testimony of Thomas Asprey. He said he saw Mary at 3.30 walking fast down Bell Lane towards Erdington. Now Bell Lane, which is now Orphanage Road, may be quite long but it isn't that long! She was about five minutes away from Hannah's yet she didn't arrive until four o'clock almost half an hour later! What was she doing, running on the spot?

Also when Hannah Cox was asked what time Mary arrived at her house she said it was about four o'clock. She was asked how she knew and she said because her mother's clock said twenty to five! Apparently her mother always kept the clock forty minutes fast so she wouldn't be late for anything!

Likewise, Thomas Broadhurst, who was the last person to see Mary alive, said he saw her about 4.20. He knew this because when he got home, which was shortly after seeing Mary, he looked at his clock. The clock read 4.40 but it was fifteen minutes fast, which meant the time was 4.25!

I think we have to put a big question mark against the times given at the trial! In Erdington in 1817, there wasn't a church clock. The nearest time source was at Aston Parish Church a mile or so away, yet people are giving the time as if they have just telephoned the Speaking Clock!

There is another very important point that we have to consider as we endeavour to unravel the mystery of Time in 1817 Erdington. When Thornton was seen at Castle Bromwich by John Haydon, Haydon knew it was five o'clock because the stable clock at Castle Bromwich Hall struck five o'clock, therefore helping to secure further Thornton's alibi.

However, I came across a rather bizarre finding. The clocks in Castle Bromwich in the early nineteenth century were fifteen minutes faster than the clocks in Erdington. Castle Bromwich kept what was known as Country time and Erdington kept Birmingham time! Therefore when the trial took place all the clocks had to be adjusted to Birmingham time. Officials went around to the witnesses' houses, noted the time and made the necessary adjustments. They also had to check the validity of the Erdington clocks. For example the officials went to Thomas Broadhurst's house and noticed that the clock read a quarter of an hour faster than Birmingham time and then it was adjusted accordingly. If however, Broadhurst, or Hannah for that matter, had either wittingly or unwittingly adjusted their clocks, then the clocks as evidence would be redundant.

When I discovered the facts about the times and clocks it took me a long time to understand it fully. However, I did find a rather large gin and tonic helped!

Whatever the outcome, the timings must be seen as unreliable. It was the re-examining of the timings that led to what could be fresh evidence in the case. One such example can be found in a letter written by Joseph Webster, who lived at Penns Hall where the inquest was held. He wrote to the magistrate William Bedford, who was busily accumulating evidence for the prosecution.

Penns.
Sunday Morning.
October 26th 1817.

My Dear Sir,

I forgot whether I mentioned to you that the statement of the Keeper that he left C. Bromwich hall at a quarter before five is disproved by Mr Rotten's maidservants. (Eliza Ray is one)

They say in consequence of its being washing day the keeper lent them his watch to rise by; that they were to call him early; they called him a quarter before five. He blamed them for doing it so late and they say that the clock must have struck five before he possibly could have left the hall. Ray is the sister-in -law of the witness Bird.

Believe me to be,

Faithfully yours,

Sgd. Joseph Webster.

The plot thickens does it not? If the letter were true, why would the keeper, John Haydon, say the clock struck five when he was still in the Hall? Likewise, why did it take Eliza Ray so long to come forward and tell her story?

Rumours mixed with fresh evidence. Some people said that the jury was "fixed" There may be an element of truth in this, as a barmaid called Elizabeth Roberts wrote a letter to Justice Bedford conveying her suspicions. Elizabeth, who worked in a Birmingham alehouse, overheard a conversation, which prompted her to write a letter. She stated that certain members of the "Twelve men good and true" which consisted of farmers and yeomen, "Were not all that they were supposed to be."

The Hon. Justice Bedford, Esquire.

Honoured Sir,

Please not to lay this letter nor the other before my Master, as he mite think I mite have spent my time better. The words which I have expressed will not surprise him, as he has often heard me repeat them to a number of his customers, respecting Clark Tandy's conduct and likewise Miss Mary Jenkins. Mr Wilson has relations that are very intimate aquaints with Thorntons, and that is Mr Jenkins at the Bulls Head, Coleshill Street, Birmingham and is the housekeeper to her uncle at Water Orton.

She had an uncle Jenkins died at Lapworth at the house called, High Chimneys, and Mr Burge married the widow, and I am well convinced that Thomas Johns and Isaac Green are well acquainted with Mr Burge. They was all three on the jury for Abraham Thornton, and what makes me think they were no better than they should be, Miss Mary Jenkins laughed and said to me, she did not doubt of his guilt, but it would not come to a hanging. Indeed, Sir, I thought that very plain language. When Miss Jenkins made her speech was very soon after Thornton was retaken.

Sir, I am your obedient and Humble servant.

Elizabeth Roberts.

I knew it wouldn't be long before the Conspiracy Theory joins us on our journey of mystery! Although Elizabeth's letter is slightly obscure, maybe to protect herself, her words "Were no better than they should be" insinuate that certain members of the jury may have committed perjury.

Is it possible, therefore, that the jurors, Clarke Tandy, Thomas Johns, Isaac Green and Joseph Burge conspired to pervert the course of justice? If so, what was their motive? There are two possible reasons. Firstly, out of loyalty to the Thornton family or purely to Thornton himself. The jurors lived locally, had a common lifestyle and maybe, as they were all men, it was a case of "the boys" sticking together. Maybe they didn't see Thornton as either a murderer or rapist but as a philanderer whose passionate actions led to dreadful crime but that Mary was somehow complicit in the tragedy. The second reason is quite simple, they were bribed! Thornton had a reputation as a ladies' man and had indeed got himself into trouble before being rescued by his father. Although not rich, he was a farmer on the Earl of Bradford's estate, with a steady income and it is possible that he used what money he did have to pay off certain members of the jury. Those jurors who may have been bribed were local farmers and may even have known Thornton Senior personally. If however, Elizabeth Roberts was mistaken there was one player on our stage that certainly wasn't all that he should have been and that was Constable Thomas Dale.

Dale's occupation was that of a Summer or 'thief catcher' belonging to the Birmingham Police Office. As we know he was the arresting officer and was responsible for taking Thornton into custody at Bordsley in Birmingham. After spending some time in Bordsley Thornton was transferred to Warwick jail and Dale was relieved of his duty. The Head Turnkey or Jailer of Warwick later gave this statement.

John Grant says he is Head Turnkey at Warwick Goal. That during the first term Thornton was in their custody he perfectly remembers seeing Dale the late Constable of Birmingham at the window in the Turnkey's room facing the felons' court yard, that Dale was leaning against the bars of the window which was open, that he walked up to the window heaved up the green blind belonging to it and then saw Thornton walking away from it towards the Hall room in the court.

It is interesting to note that at this particular stage of writing Dale is described as the late constable. Fear not, this was not an apparition but it is Grant's way of saying that Dale was no longer a member of the orders of law and order. Soon after the first trial he was dismissed for improper conduct! Grant continues in his statement,

That Dale being a Constable he used to take the liberty of going into the Turnkey's room when he chose it but it was not a room in which strangers are allowed to enter because it is communicated with the felon's yard.

Had Dale made some sort of pact with Thornton? It certainly seems so. Let us go back to the Tyburn House where Dale met Thornton for the first time. When Dale examined Thornton's clothing there was blood on his shirt. It was at this point that Thornton admits he had sex with Mary. However, Dale implied at the trial that Thornton had told him this before he had seen the blood. Was it possible that Thornton only realised the blood was there for the first time when he undressed in front of Dale? To aid his story that sex with Mary was with consent he told Dale to say that he admitted intercourse with her **BEFORE** the blood was discovered. The transcript of the trial makes interesting reading. Mr Reader cross-examined Dale,

"Did he confess to you that he had had a connection with the deceased before he was taken to be examined?"

Dale replied, "Yes, he did. I believe he did."

"Did anyone hear it beside yourself?"

"I can hardly tell, I think not. I do not recollect that anybody was present at the time"

"Did you tell Mr Bedford what the prisoner had said before he examined him?"

"No, I believe not."

It seems either Dale found being a witness a daunting experience or that he was being deliberately vague. When re-examined by the prosecution by Mr Sergeant Copley, Dale seems to falter.

"Did the prisoner tell you that he had connection with the deceased before the magistrate came to Clarke's?"

Dale responded with, "I'm not sure whether he said so before or after."

Copley pressed Dale further. "You are sure he did say so to you, are you?"

Dale replied, "I'm quite sure he said so, when we were searching him upstairs."

Copley with emphasis asked Dale again, "Are you quite sure of that?"

Dale replied, "Yes."

In his vagueness Dale gives two different accounts to the prosecution and to the defence! Also there is evidence of collusion between Dale and Thornton at the Inquest that took place at Webster's home, Penns Hall. The evidence comes from a young apprentice.

John Collingwood, Apprentice to Mr Barlow, Cabinetmaker in Birmingham, says

that on Friday the 30th May last he was at Mr Webster's house at Penn's Mill being one of the days on which the Inquest of the body of Mary Ashford was held. That before the Inquest sat he went into the room where Thornton was and stood immediately behind him. Dale, the constable, sat exactly opposite to him about a yard from him. At this time Mr Saddler, the Attorney, came into the room and whispered to Thornton in the hearing of the witness, "Am I to do what I can for you?" Thornton answered, "You have seen my Father?" Saddler said, "Yes, be sure and hold fast." That Mr Saddler then left the room and in about two minutes after, Dale and Thornton put their heads together and Thornton whispered to Dale in witness's hearing, "Saddler says I must hold fast and by God it won't do to own to it." Dale made no immediate answer, but in about five minutes after, whispered to Thornton and Thornton to Dale but what they said witness could not hear them.

(Sgd.) John Collingwood.

It must be remembered that Dale was an officer of the law and was supposed to be impartial and neutral! Collingwood's statement was also used as fresh evidence that was going to be presented at the second trial. Whatever Dale's motives in establishing a relationship with Thornton and siding with him, they were enough for William Bedford to write to Lord Sidmouth.

"...Being firmly persuaded that he, (Dale) grossly perjured himself in a very important part of the evidence on the trial of Thornton on which Mr Justice Holroyd laid great stress in his charge to the jury, and in a great measure led to his acquittal. In consequence of this gross misconduct, I requested a full attendance of my Brother Magistrate at the Police Office on the Monday after the Assizes; and after a minute investigation of the facts he was immediately dismissed from the Police Office with great disgrace."

Bedford was spearheading the campaign to gather fresh evidence in order to bring about a successful prosecution. When Thornton was originally arrested, Bedford took it upon himself to visit him at the jail in Birmingham. Bedford was furious with Thornton and asked him how he had the impudence to deny the killing of Mary. He was also astonished that Thornton was able to eat after such a wicked act had taken place. Bedford in his anger told Thornton that not only would he hang but that his body would be given to surgery to be dissected and that he long deserved his fate. Furthermore, he had already cost his father several hundred pounds to get him out of such scrapes but he wouldn't be able to rely on his father's money to save him this time. Bedford's anger was so strong that his language was described as reproachable and his behaviour was, "very unbecoming a gentleman and a magistrate."

It is also Bedford that brings us to the attention of one Omar Hall. Omar Hall was in Warwick Gaol awaiting transportation as he had fallen on hard times. He hailed from Milford, Stafford and had married a Miss Goodwin also of Milford,

Stafford. He was a banker but became a victim of misfortune, so much so that he had to turn to crime. He was caught and convicted of stealing fowl. Although it was his first offence it seemed violence was involved. Maybe he resisted arrest. Whatever were the circumstances, the judge who tried him sentenced him to transportation.

Hall and Thornton became companions whilst in jail. Grant put in his statement;

"He, (Grant) had often seen Thornton walking in the court yard with Homer Hall* whom Thornton seemed to find upon as his principal companion."

Hall later stated that in one of the conversations with Thornton that he told him in confidence that he had murdered Mary Ashford.

* Sometimes Omar Hall is referred to as Homer Hall.

Bedford was suspicious of Omar Hall's sudden declaration. In the same letter to Lord Sidmouth he writes,

My Lord,

I happened to be in Birmingham when I read your Lordship's communication respecting Abraham Thornton, with the statement made by Omar Hall of the conversations that passed between him and Thornton in Warwick Gaol, though it appears extraordinary and indeed suspicious that he should not have given this information sooner....

Despite his suspicions of Hall, Bedford certainly thought it would be worthwhile to pursue the matter further. In his letter to Lord Sidmouth he says;

My nephew is in Town for the purpose of prosecuting the Writ of Appeal against Thornton and will have the honour of waiting upon your Lordship to inform you of the material facts of this unhappy case, which has excited a greater degree of interest (I may say) throughout the Kingdom, than any I ever heard of.

I shall be much obliged to your Lordship if you will allow my nephew to have an interview with Omar Hall. I have shortly mentioned to him the crime for which he was transported and should he be instrumental in giving information to satisfy the object of public justice in bringing Thornton to trial, I have no doubt that your Lordship will procure him a free pardon to enable to give his evidence.

I have the honour to be, My Lord, Your Lordship's most obedient servant.

William Bedford. Birches Green November 4th 1817.

Hall was interviewed as he lay on board a convict ship called the "Justicia," which was moored at Woolwich. He was interviewed, however not by Bedford's nephew but by John Capper who states;

"Yesterday I went on board the "Justicia," and saw the prisoner, Omar Hall who delivered to me and signed in my presence, the accompanying written statement and although the greater part of what he stated appears to have been conversation, between himself and Thornton, when together in Warwick Gaol; yet in a case of such Atrocity, I beg leave to submit for your consideration whether it would not be proper to transmit the same or a copy thereof to William Bedford, Esq., an active magistrate at Birmingham..."

John Capper's letter was written a day before Bedford sent his to Lord Sidmouth. Capper had heard of Omar Hall through John Grant who had now moved to London. It seems at times that the whole legal profession was involved in this tragic case eager it seems to prove Thornton's guilt. Homer Hall was a willing participant. He told Capper the following whilst languishing in jail with Thornton as he awaited his trial at Warwick.

"Thornton soon after being committed to Warwick, knowing my former situation in life, much coverted my acquaintance; and, sleeping in the same cell in the prison, very frequently advised me as to his case, and, at times, opened his mind very freely to me on the subject."

William Bedford and his supporters no doubt welcomed what Hall had to say regarding Thornton's confessional period when, "He opened his mind."

"He confessed to have committed the rape, and said in what way it was done, which is too brutish to name. In regard to the murder he never fully confessed to putting her in to the pit in a living state, although in all his transactions and conversation signified to me that he had done so in a dead one."

Existing for so long in such dark, damp conditions and with an uncertain future Thornton obviously needed a confidant and obviously felt he could trust Hall. After all, until his misfortune visited him Hall had been a respectable and prosperous banker by all accounts. Thornton also knew that whatever he said could be denied and that a convicted felon, as Hall was, would not have the right to give evidence in a court of law. However, according to Hall he confided in him the following,

"For soon after being committed he having information that his shoe mark as well as the print of his breeches knees would be very much against him, he asked for my opinion on the subject. I very freely said, if they had, it would, and very much so, and named two cases, the one at Stafford eight years back, a man for shooting his brother through a window and convicted upon the evidence of two large nails in the heel of the shoe near to the window. And in the case of Brindley at Warwick for the murder of a female by putting her into a pit and drowning of her in the way he had done, and convicted by a patch being set crossways on the breeches knee of a pair of corded breeches and the print of which was proved at the edge of the pit. If that was the case with his, he had better prepare himself for the awful day. He replied he need not on that account as it could not be in such a way as to convict him, as the nails in his shoe was so small that they could not possible make a print as any man could swear to, as it was turfed where he stepped, and as for the print on the

breeches knee, could not be the case, as he never was on them, except with the girl, and her petticoats was under them, and said, in his own opinion he had nothing to fear but the evidence of Dale the Constable."

Yet again Dale is involved in the shady dealings that Thornton is apparently involved in. In order to gain his liberty. Omar Hall continues,

"He had nothing to fear but the evidence of Dale the constable, who took him into custody, as he had named something to him which must operate against him, but had promised, when at Birmingham that he would not name it nor produce a handkerchief, I believe for the use of the pocket. And some blood that was on the sleeve of the shirt near to the hand, he did not mind the tail part, and that his father was to settle that with him, but should shortly know, and his mind would be at ease."

If we are to accept Hall's version then not only is Dale suspected of committing perjury, accepting bribes, but that he is guilty of concealing material evidence. The handkerchief must have had Mary's blood on it, which suggests that he used it to wipe her blood from his hands. Having blood on his shirtsleeve indicates that his hands and arms were in contact with Mary's genitals and that is how the blood got on the cloth. It also suggests that force were used. Hall carries on to emphasis the involvement of Thornton's father.

"Soon after some person called him to the window. On his return I asked him who had been to see him. He said it was Dale. I said I suppose he wished to get something more out of him, as those kind of men seldom came to a prisoner for anything else. He said he was his friend and said his father had settled that matter with him that he had named to me."

Hall also states in his letter that he lent Thornton a pen, ink, paper and wax to write a letter to Dale. A week afterwards Dale paid Thornton another visit. Hall eavesdropped on the conversation,

"I heard Dale call Thornton back and say in a low tone of voice, 'I say I shall not want to see you again and I hope you will perform your promise on your liberty and you will find me to do the same as agreed.' On his return seeing me so near the window said he hoped Dale did not see me there. If so, all would have been up and had the pleasure to say all was settled."

Shortly before Thornton's trial Omar Hall was taken to London to await transportation. He concludes in his account,

"I was suddenly sent off to this place about a week or ten days before the Assizes. He had just time to speak to me and hoped I would say nothing of what was past, although I fully intended had I stopped till the Assizes."

With Hall about to be sent to Australia, vital evidence being suppressed, and having secured his liberty Thornton must have thought the gods were on his side. However, The "Writ of Appeal" was carried through and Thornton did have something more to fear than just Dale's evidence."

Chapter Twelve. Castle Bromwich. October 1817.

It was a Thursday night when we arrived at Castle Bromwich. Autumn was with us once again and there was a slight chill in the air. Mr Bedford, the magistrate had requested me, John Hackney, to go to Castle Bromwich and collect Thornton, along with my two companions, Thomas Martin and Jonathan Baker. We left Birmingham about seven o'clock that evening. It took us just over the hour to reach Castle Bromwich, a place I don't know that well to be honest.

When we got there we went to Barton's Public House. There were a few old men in there drinking pots of ale and a good fire was lit, which we were grateful for as it had turned quite blustery outside and you feel it more in Castle Bromwich being on a hill and all.

Abraham Thornton's farmhouse, Castle Bromwich, now Shard End.

We took the Landlord to one side and told him of our business. Told him that we needed some one to show us the Thornton household. The Landlord said one of the old men would show us. He came with us and showed us the farmhouse. I could see a lamp burning and as it was a moonlit night could see the smoke coming from the chimney.

I told Martin and Baker to wait outside and I would call them if I needed them. I went up to the door and knocked, a servant girl soon opened the door.

I said, "Is Mr Thornton at home?"

"Why Mr Thornton's abed but you can come in and speak to the mistress."

I realized then that I should have stated my business clearer as I am certain she meant did I want to see the old man and not young Thornton. She led me into the kitchen where I saw Abraham Thornton sitting by the fire with his mother. Another servant, a man, was also in the kitchen. I said to young Thornton,

"How do you do?"

"I suppose you mean my father, sir?" came the reply.

"No sir, I do not. I wish to speak to you."

"I will be glad of it," Thornton replied.

He got up and invited me into the little parlour, which was modest but pleasant.

"I think you know why I have come," I said quite plainly to him.

"I do," he said with his face looking slightly downcast.

He then asked me to read the warrant, which I did. After I finished reading it to him he said.

"Two gentlemen came to see me today, to inform me that William Ashford was called up on Tuesday evening at twelve o'clock to go to London. They told me I had time to leave to be off with myself but I said, 'No. I won't go. I'll stay and see this business out.' I am surprised Mr Hackney that you have come to me so soon."

I asked no questions of him but only stated that it was time to go. We went into the kitchen and by this time Martin and Baker had come into the house. We all stood there when Thornton's mother threw up her arms and exclaimed,

"That cruel Mr Bedford." She looked to her son.

"What does he want with him. Isn't he satisfied now?"

She added in a most sarcastic tone, "We must thank him for all this."

Thornton looked at us and said, "You'll be satisfied only when you have my life." He slowly turned round and said to his Mother, "Mother, make yourself easy for I have made up my mind. I will go with them and see it through."

I handcuffed him after he put his coat on and we then took him to the Bradford Arms in Castle Bromwich. Thornton asked if he could call upon several friends as he was going away from home and may not see them again but I wouldn't allow it. It doesn't pay to be soft of heart in this job. His friends could have set about us and allowed Thornton to escape. We immediately returned to Birmingham and we did not stay anywhere on the road.

On our way back he insisted that he didn't murder the poor girl and kept on saying that if he had not gone with her none of this would have happened. He repeated this several times. He admitted having connection with her but that she was as willing as he was.

When we got to Birmingham Baker left us and Martin and I continued to Warwick. On the road to Warwick Martin said to him,

"It's a pity that you didn't take off for America as soon as the trial was over."

Thornton replied, "If I knew as much as I do now I would be in America by now."

When we got to Warwick a man called Dale came to see the prisoner but he was refused admittance.

Chapter Thirteen. St Winifred's Vicarage.

I remember watching News at 10.00 one night and thinking, Wouldn't it be rather odd if the man on the television screen suddenly said, "And today, 'Abraham Thornton was taken from Birmingham to stand trial in London at Westminster Hall.'

Well, that's what happened soon after he was arrested by Hackney and his companions and the news spread through the country. Even without the medium of television it went as fast as it could in the early part of the nineteenth century. He was taken to Marshalsea prison in the east of London and on the seventeenth of November stood trial at Westminster Hall. The case had caught the imagination of the Nation and Thornton had become infamous.

After languishing in prison, the day came and Thornton left the damp, squalid conditions of the Marshalsea and was escorted to Westminster. Such was the infamy of the case that the London mob was out to do justice. Such was the fury of that band of citizens that Thornton had to be smuggled into the court via the back door!

Lord Chief Justice Ellenborough presided with other judges who took their seats early in the morning to hear the case.

William Ashford was called forward. A contemporary account for the proceedings described him as,

"A plain, country young man, about twenty two years of age, of short stature, sandy hair, and blue eyes."

The Appeal was read out and Thornton was asked if he was guilty or not guilty of the wilful murder of the said Mary Ashford, "whereof he stood appealed."

There was a brief silence then something quite startling happened. Thornton walked onto the courtroom floor and stated quite clearly, "I am not guilty and I am ready to defend myself with my body." At the same time he reached into a bag provided by his Counsel. To everyone's astonishment in the court he produced a pair of gauntlets. They were made of leather and were the type horsemen used. He put one on his left hand as he was uttering the challenge and the other he threw on the courtroom floor. It was like a scene out of medieval times when knights fought duels and this was precisely what Thornton was doing. He was issuing a challenge to William Ashford!

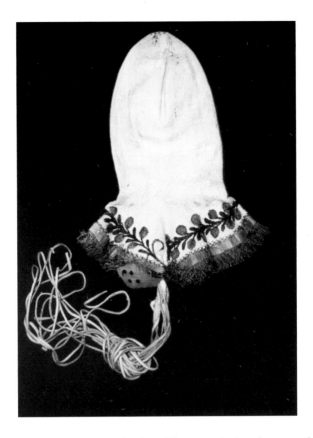

Gauntlet thrown down by Abraham Thornton during the second trial.

The court and those in the public gallery were both shocked and amazed at Thornton's actions. The lawyers, learned as they were, did not know what to do. Thornton had thrown down the gauntlet and had issued what was termed, "Wager of battel." It was a former law of the Normans and was STILL law as it had never been repealed and the last wager of battel had taken place in 1638.

If it was law then William Ashford had the choice of either picking up the gauntlet or not. If he picked up the gauntlet he accepted the challenge and would have to fight Thornton. If he didn't then Thornton was able to walk away from the court a free man. What would have been the procedure if Ashford took up the challenge? Apparently it would have been as follows;

'*If the appellant took up the glove, the defendant would lay his right hand on the Gospels, and taking hold of the appellant's hand with his left, would swear that he did not commit the murder. The appellant with the same formula would assert the guilt of the defendant. The lists, wherein the battle was to be fought were to be sixty feet square, the sides being duly squared with the four cardinal points. On the day appointed the court would proceed to the lists from Westminster Hall, the judges being fully robed; and proclamation would be made for the combatants, who would be required to appear with bare head, arms and leg, each of them to be furnished with batons, tipped with horn, and with a leathern shield or target and declare an oath that they had in their possession neither, "Bone, stone or grass." In other words no sort of witches' charms. "Whereby the law of God may be depressed and the law of the Devil exalted."*

They were then to fight until the stars appeared, unless one of them were previously vanquished. If the appellant were vanquished, or if the defendant was able to continue the fight until the stars appeared, he was free, and the appellant would be subject to a year's prison and a fine. If the appellant turned craven and gave up the fight, he became infamous and lost the privileges of a free man. If on the other hand the defendant should be vanquished, he was to be instantly executed.'

Thornton's physique was much stronger and more powerful than Ashford's. It would be like Mike Tyson getting into the ring with Norman Wisdom! Ashford's lawyers complained that to apply the law would be both unjust and inhumane. They also lodged the complaint that; "Wager by battel" could only be used in cases where there was circumstantial evidence of the crime but could not be used if the evidence was conclusive of guilt. Ashford's lawyers felt that there was sufficient new evidence to ascertain Thornton's guilt and therefore he should be denied the entitlement of this ancient law.

However, Judge Ellenborough and his colleagues took a different view. They had been unhappy with the "Writ of Appeal" in the first place as it suggested that there had been either a miscarriage of justice in the first trial or incompetence had taken place. The judiciary was also slightly worried what the consequences of the battle would be, as it could easily have become a unique spectacle for Londoners to marvel at. Also the judges felt that, as the writ of appeal was an obsolete law why then shouldn't Thornton have access to another obsolete law! The court allowed the challenge to stand and Ashford withdrew his Appeal and Abraham Thornton walked free for the second time. The Ashford family once again faced disappointment and grief.

The case aroused both interest and curiosity amongst the people of England. Pamphlets were printed and were divided in opinion as to whether Thornton was guilty or not. The trial was published **IN EXTENSO** and portraits of Mary and Abraham were on sale everywhere. There was also an engraving of the Fatal Field showing the footprints of Mary and her alleged murderer. Mr Samuel Lines of Birmingham published a very strange looking drawing, which, when it was held up to the light revealed a trail of blood!

So Thornton was the last man to walk free for the second time for a crime in England. The following year "Appeal of Murder" and "Wager of battel" were taken off the statute books.

Almost two weeks before the trial the country had been plunged into mourning. On November the sixth, the original date for the trial, the very popular Princess Charlotte died. For the Ashford family, their own "Princess" had not only died but was also a victim of the English legal system for the second time.

Chapter Fourteen. Hannah Cox's cottage, Erdington. 1817.

I can't rightly remember what I was doing when the news came from London that Thornton was at liberty again. My Mother told me when I came back from Mr Machin's. It was already dark, being November. The leaves were still falling and quite a wind was blowing. The news came from the London coach. It soon spread and it was if the whole village was in mourning again. I met Daniel Clarke and he told me that Thornton would have to still stay in London but he was coming back to Castle Bromwich even if he was the most infamous man in England. He had made Mary famous all right but for all the wrong reasons. They've even written plays about her. One is called, "The Murdered Maid; or The Clock struck four." Then there's another, "The Mysterious Murder, or What's the clock!" I haven't seen them. I don't think I want to.

A lot of people round here think I had something to do with it. First they said why did I send Benjamin back to the Tyburn. I told them it was to get my bracelet. They said I just said that so I would let Thornton and Mary be alone together. Then they say I deliberately said it was four o'clock to help Thornton have an account for himself. They say it was me who saved him from the gallows. Then other folk said what I said at the inquest was different from what I said at the trial to make sure Thornton was found guilty. I wish people would make up their mind. Some other folk said it wasn't Thornton at all but my Ben! They say he was secretly in love with Mary and after seeing me as far as the lane that night he pretended to go home but really he secretly followed them. God knows why, but so the gossip goes. He spent most of the night hiding in the bushes and after he watched them connect, he waited for her, and when she got back, fell into a rage and threw her into the pit! What nonsense! When I heard it I didn't know whether to laugh or cry.

Thornton did come back by all accounts in April but I never saw him. I met Daniel round harvest time and he said that Thornton had gone to America. His father had died and is buried up on Castle Hill. Died of a broken heart, they say, as all the bother over the past year took its toll and killed him. Daniel also said that when he got to Liverpool he was supposed to gain passage on a certain ship but when the crew and all found out who he was they refused to sail with him on board! He had to get passage on an Irish ship called the SS Shamrock. No one has heard of him since he sailed.

The village is more or less as it was now all the trials and tribulations are over. Oh, I can start calling it a village as they are going to build a chapel here on the High Street near to the Roebuck Inn. So Erdington will be a proper village after all these years. It's a pity Mary won't see it. She could have got married in that chapel. She would have made a lovely bride. She could have come to my wedding. Yes, after all this time Mr Carter has promised to make an honest woman of me. We're getting wed soon and then we'll be leaving. Ben says he can get a farm east of Erdington at Nuneaton. I hope we are happy.

I shall never forget Mary and I thought what they wrote on her headstone was only right and fitting.

Chapter Fifteen. St Winifred's Vicarage.

On one of my rare days off I drove up to Birmingham and visited Sutton churchyard. I had been before and it is worth a visit. In front of the church lies the well laid out Vesey Memorial Gardens. There are steps that lead to the church. The church is quite high up and the churchyard is surrounded by a decorated brick wall that belongs more to a castle than an English churchyard. There are few free upstanding headstones and all of them lie against the churchyard walls. There is the occasional tomb, black with age, guarded by railings, which lies near the path that leads to the church.

Mary's grave looks like an old slab of stone as it's terribly worn away. I put some flowers on it and said a prayer for her. I remember staring for a while and then looking up at the sprawling town of Sutton Coldfield still full of shoppers. "A bit different now," I thought to myself at the time. I also wondered what it was like that June day when she was buried. What was the weather like? Was everyone dressed in black huddled around the open grave? Did anyone sing a lament? The Reverend Luke Booker the vicar of Dudley organized a fund for the headstone and inscription, which was raised by public subscription. It reads;

As a warning to female virtue and a humble monument to female chastity this stone marks the grave of,

MARY ASHFORD

Who in the 20th year of her age
Having incautiously repaired to a scene of amusement without proper protection was brutally violated and murdered on the 27th May 1817.

Lovely and chaste as is the Primrose pale.
Rifled of virgin sweetness by the gale.
Mary! The wretch who thee remorseless slew,
Avenging Wrath, which sleeps not, will persue,
For though the deed of blood be veiled in Night,
Will not the judge of all the Earth do right?
Fair blighted flower! The Muse that weeps thy doom
Rears o'er thy murdered Form this warning tomb!

*Mary Ashford's Grave, Holy Trinity Church,
Sutton Coldfield before falling into disrepair.*

Luke Booker's words summed up the feelings of both Mary's family and all those
that lived in Erdington and the surrounding countryside. They were powerless to act
especially as Thornton had walked free for a second time. In order to seek justice
Booker called upon, "The Judge of all the Earth."

To my knowledge people still visit the grave. I came across an article that was
written in 1967. The writer of the article said that around 1957 he visited Mary's
grave one Whitsun holiday to see if the inscription could still be read. The grave
stone at this point was still horizontal. When he visited the grave there was a jam jar
with flowers in it and a brief note which said, "With love to Mary, not forgotten."
The writer thought it was signed, "Bill and Joan." I think it is a pity that the
inscription has gone and maybe it would be a good idea if some sort of public fund
were started to pay for it.

So Mary lay cold in the grave and Thornton was America bound.

Chapter Sixteen. Liverpool. September 1818.

The young woman had just returned from walking along the harbourside. She stood
on the narrowed cobbled lane and looked back out to sea. The night sky slowly met
the horizon of the grey deep waters. There was a chill in the air as the wind blew

across the waters making the sea choppy and turbulent. The sound of seagulls spread across the skies. She could still make out the rusting blocks of metal wrapped with thick brown ropes that hold the small fishing vessels that bobbed up and down by the harbour wall.

She pulled her shawl over her shoulders to keep out the cold. The shawl covered the old, slightly tattered embroidered dress she was wearing. It seemed too small on first appearance as her breasts spilt over the fine starched material. She looked once more out to sea and searched the horizon. Her eyes stopped at the sight of a sailing ship in the distance. All her sails were up as she slowly crossed the Irish Sea. The girl stood on the cobbled lane. The tavern sign, "The Lamb and Flag," swung in the sea breeze. She kept watch until the ship disappeared into the evening light. She opened her shawl and pulled out a letter with a broken seal. She reflected on what had happened the previous night and how she would put it in words if she were ever asked.

"I live in the shadows of the streets, winter and summer, six days a week, waiting for them. When I hear them I step out of the shadows and give them the prettiest smile I can muster. 'And what can I do for you sir?' I say as if he were a gentleman who had a title and all. Most of them are just drunken scum. I have entertained the scum of the world.

Some come because they are so full of drink they think there are the world's greatest lovers, others tell such tales about how their wives have deserted the marital bed and that they will die if they don't connect soon. They smell of stale ale and handle me no better than a beast. They are always rough, grunting like pigs and often they leave me with bruises or marks.

I remember seeing him. There was something about him that made me think he was different. I walked out in front of him and I gave him such a fright. He didn't seem interested at first but when I put my arm through his arm and said, 'Let's walk a little.' He came with me as if he were a lamb. We went down an alley and I stopped and began to undo his coat. He stopped me straight away and said, 'No. Not here.' He was more considerate than most so we went to a tavern, 'The Lamb and Flag' and took a room.

I asked him why he was in Liverpool and he told me that he was off to America but his ship had been delayed and that he would be going the next day on the evening tide on a ship called the Shamrock. A good Irish ship I told him, which made him laugh. I stared at him and lifted the candle closer to his face. 'Don't I know you?' I said. His dark eyes peered back at me and he said, 'No' and without a further word scrambled out of bed. He took a chamber pot and went to relieve himself. As he carried out his call of nature I noticed his breeches hanging over the bed. I also noticed that there was a large piece of paper sticking out. I don't know what made me do it but I pulled it out of his pocket and quickly hid it under the pillow of the bed. He came back and said very little, except what some of them say, and that is, 'Thank you.' Well, it's better than having a beating as some of them do or escape without handing over the money. He was generous all right but now he looked worried.

As he left the room I said to him, 'Good Luck in America, Sir.'

He turned and smiled but said nothing and walked out the door. I retrieved the letter from the pillow and began to read it. On my Mother's life I have never read anything like it before."

Chapter Seventeen. St Winifred's Vicarage.

The letter is quite extraordinary. It never came to light until the 1930's and then it was a question **ABOUT** the letter but not actually the letter. Someone wrote to a Liverpool newspaper stating that when Thornton was in Liverpool he visited a prostitute. Fortunately, it doesn't go into graphic detail but it did say that the prostitute, who ever she was, stole a letter from Thornton. When she read the letter it told of his guilt. He plainly admitted to killing Mary.

The story goes that Thornton intended to deposit the letter at the Customs House with instructions that it be sent to Castle Bromwich. He knew that when the letter was sent he would be safely out at sea. In those days there weren't any international agreements between countries and the exchange of suspected felons. Also by the time he was out of English waters what were they to do? Send the navy after him?

I don't know if the story is true or not but if it is why did it take so long to come to light and why didn't the girl take it to the relevant authorities immediately? I suppose, even if she did hand the letter over to someone in authority, legally what could they do? After all he had been freed from a court of law twice!

Another version of the story is that on reading the letter the prostitute black mailed him and he paid her handsomely to buy her silence. Whichever is true, that is twice now that we have come across alleged confessions from Thornton, the first being the oral report of Omar Hall and now from a lady of the night. Whether it be true or not, sadly, it was very doubtful that a convicted felon and a prostitute would be believed and that their motives were truly altruistic. However, we do know that Thornton did board a ship bound for America. Aris's Birmingham Gazette printed on the 25th October 1818 the following,

It was stated a few weeks since, that Abraham Thornton had arrived in Liverpool for the purpose of emigrating to the United States. It appears, however, that he experienced some difficulty in securing a passage thither. He had engaged a berth in the 'Independence' but when other passengers became acquainted with his name and character, they unanimously refused to go in the same vessel with him, and a new muster-roll was in consequence made out, in which his name was omitted."

This gave him time to 'visit' a prostitute and maybe she did steal that letter but he was still America bound. The Gazette reported a week later on November the third,

We are informed on good authority that Abraham Thornton succeeded in securing a passage to America in the ship, 'Shamrock.' And that he sailed from Liverpool on the thirtieth of September 1818.

So, it seems Mr Thornton has survived the most extraordinary of fates! He sailed off to America and he was never heard of again - or was he?"

Chapter Eighteen. The State of Maryland, United States of America. 1862.

U.S Marshall Tyrone Lewis looked up at the hot midday sun. He mopped his brow with the blue and white cloth before replacing it around his neck. He pulled the brim of his hat down, shook the reigns of his chestnut mare and cantered across the wide green meadows of Maryland.

He rode for several miles and enjoyed the steady, calm journey. However, he had to be vigilant. The war had just started and Confederate forces were on the move. Although he was in one of the safe States of the Union, rumour had it that the rebels would disguise themselves as Union soldiers and cause as much mischief as possible. The Marshall had only heard last night in Baltimore that there was even a plot to kill the president, Abraham Lincoln.

He pulled a pocket watch out of his waistcoat and flicked it open. After checking the time he looked up towards the sky and noticed that clouds were beginning slowly to cover the heat of the sun. The clouds soon darkened the sky.

"Don't want to get caught out in a storm," he muttered to himself. He only went a mile or so on when he came across a man coming towards him driving a wagon. The Marshall put his hand up and the old man pulled the brake on the wagon and pulled the horse to a halt.

"Am I on the right road to Black Hawk Hall?" the Marshall asked.

"Yes sir," came the reply from the white bearded man who looked slightly anxious.

"It's about a mile up the road. You'll see some evergreens and cattle grazing. Then there's a kind of track that leads to the hall. Can I ask who wants to know?"

"You can. Tyrone Lewis, US Marshall."

"You're going to Black Hawk?"

But before Tyrone could answer the old man said, "You may be too late, Marshall, as Mr Hyde died only a few days ago."

"I ain't come to see Mr Hyde. I've come to see his widow Mrs Hyde."

"Something ain't right up at the house is it? I always said to Merry, that's my wife, that things weren't right up there. I know the old Mr Hyde kept himself to himself but there was something not quite right."

"And what would that be?" came the Marshall's laconic reply.

"He still had his English accent."

"It's not against the law to have an English accent." The Marshall quipped.

"Sure I know that. It's just…"

"Just what?"

"Well, I have heard stories."

"Oh yeah, what kind of stories?"

"How he got to have a hall and so many cattle."

"I heard that he earned it honestly running fishing boats in Baltimore. Now if you've heard different I think you ought to tell me considering I'm the law round here."

"Well, like I said, they were just stories I heard."

"Well, let's keep it that way shall we?" At that point he raised his hat and ushered the horse into motion. The old man gave a weak smile and touched the brim of his hat. Tyrone rode on. At least the old man had been right with his directions. As he crossed the brow of the hill he saw some gates and the dirt track that led up to the hall. "It sure ain't no palace," Tyrone thought to himself, "But it's bigger than most folk would have." As he rode down the track he noticed small clouds of smoke come from the chimney.

"Well, at least some one is home." He said with a sigh of relief.

A pleasant looking, kind faced black woman called Martha greeted him. He entered the house. "So this is Black Hawk Hall." He said to himself as he gazed around looking at the fine polished wooden furniture. He was left in the lobby and as he waited all that could be heard was the ticking of the large grandfather clock in the corner. He walked over to the clock and next to it was a model of a sailing ship. He leant down towards it and noticed that there was an inscription written on it, SS Shamrock.

It wasn't long before the Marshall was sitting in the Parlour with Mrs Hyde, and her son and daughter. Martha the maid had also joined them. She had also made sure that Tyrone had been well fed with homemade steak pie and some cool beer. Likewise his chestnut mare had been taken to the stable for a well-deserved nosebag.

Mrs Hyde was appropriately dressed in black and sat at the head of the table. Her son who was dressed in the uniform of the US army sat at her right hand side and held her hand. The daughter, also dressed in black, sat opposite the Marshall. Martha stood by the door. There was silence and chinks of light came through into the shuttered room. The son leant forward and turned up the light in one of the several oil lamps in the room.

Mrs Hyde began to speak.

"I should like to thank Marshall Lewis formally for coming today all the way from Baltimore, especially travelling alone when the country is in such danger. However, as we all know, my husband, your father, died after suffering so much. Long before he died he gave me this key."

All the occupants of the room looked at the ornate metal key that Mrs Hyde held in her hand. She continued,

" This is the key for a box my husband gave to me many years ago. My husband left me plain instructions that the box was to be opened after his death. He also requested that a member of the country's law enforcement be present. That is why Marshall Lewis is with us today."

She gave a wry smile to Tyrone who replied with a simple, "Mam."

"I would like very much if Marshall Lewis would open the box." Tyrone nodded. Mrs Hyde passed him the key. He leant over the table reached the box, which he brought towards himself. The lid of the box sprang open. All eyes were fixed on the box.

"Please, Marshall continue."

Tyrone took out an old parchment that was wrapped with a red ribbon. He undid the ribbon and gently unfolded the parchment. He began to read in silence.

"Well, " the young soldier said impatiently.

"I'm afraid, Mrs Hyde, or should I say Mrs Thornton, I have some bad news for you.

Martha burst into tears.

Chapter Nineteen. St Winifred's Vicarage

I have a small old metal box, which, when opened, plays an Italian tune; a tune which everyone knows, as most ice cream vans blare it out every day in summer but no one never seems to know its name. When I look at that box I think of the dying Thornton in Black Hawk Hall all those miles away in America. Also was it just a story that became part of folklore? In this case there is a modicum of historical fact.

A letter published in the Sutton News circa 1888 said that Thornton indeed died at a place called Black Hawk Hall and that upon his death a metal box was opened and the contents revealed what was deemed as 'Tantamount to a confession'.

The letter also stated that Thornton had arrived at New York, and after going through immigration made his way to Baltimore in Maryland. I suppose there is a hint of irony that after being freed twice on the charge of murdering a girl called Mary he travelled thousands of miles to live in a place called Maryland!

He must have maintained contact with his family because it is recorded in several sources that he settled in Maryland and that he was successful in business, as he owned several fishing boats. He also married and had a son and a daughter. Recent research has indicated that his son was killed in the American Civil War and that his daughter died after contracting tuberculosis. It is thought that he died circa 1860 just as the war was breaking out. What is fascinating, and this only came to light recently was the fact written in the Sutton News that he died in a place called Black Hawk Hall. However, despite research no one including myself, has been able to locate Black Hawk Hall. The Victorian writer stated quite clearly that he died at Black Hawk Hall but failed to mention where exactly Black Hawk Hall was! It is only a conjecture that it is in Maryland, as by all accounts it was Maryland that Thornton went to.

Oh yes, there's a lot of information about Black Hawk. He was an Indian Chief, or to be correct, a Native American Chief. He fought for the British in the 1812 War of Independence. However, he was betrayed by them and was later killed. The battles he fought were to the west of the Mississippi, near the Great Lakes, which is nowhere near Maryland! Black Hawk's remains were kept in the 'DelaCroix Museum,' until they were destroyed in a fire.

Either for some reason or another there was a house named after Black Hawk in Maryland or the Black Hawk Hall he died in wasn't in Maryland but some where west of the Mississippi. For some reason and I don't know why, the state of Wisconsin springs to mind! Looking for Thornton and Black Hawk Hall is akin to looking for the proverbial needle in a haystack! Also in my opinion it is almost certain that he changed his surname adopting his mother's maiden name, which is Hyde.

Another interesting feature about Black Hawk Hall came about when I was invited to talk about the case for the BBC. I was asked to talk on BBC local radio in Birmingham one Sunday morning and afterwards a lady rang me at the vicarage. She said that her family name was Thornton and that before the Second World War her aunt told her of a black box that had been deposited with the family. It was never opened and no one knows the whereabouts of either the box or its contents. She wanted to know if there was a connection!

The case of Mary and Abraham has been unsolved now for nearly two hundred years. It has fascinated historians, journalists and sleuths for over three centuries. I was looking at some papers the other day in the library when I came across a gentleman called Sir John Hall, who obviously took a great interest in the case. He lived in London during the 1920's. The decade evokes images of the Roaring Twenties. Black and white films of smiling girls with short hair and slim fitting dresses that had never been shorter. Then there was the dance music when everyone seemed to dance to the "Charleston." Then there are images of feathers and flappers, talking movies, P.G Wodehouse, Agatha Christie and afternoon tea at the Ritz! A lady American pilot, Amelia Earhart, flew solo across the Atlantic. They were exciting and refreshing times after the pointless waste and carnage of the First World War. However, for many of our citizens it was also the decade of the General Strike and great poverty and misery, which summons up images of that great crusade, the walk from Jarrow. Times indeed were changing but for Sir John living in London his thoughts were with Mary and the England of 1817!

Chapter Twenty. London 1924.

Sir John Hall yawned as he walked down the hallway of his London apartment in Dorset Square. There was a slight chill in the air but his woollen dressing gown and cosy slippers kept out the cold. He leant down and picked up his morning copy of "The Daily Express," along with the morning post.

He walked back into the dining room carrying his paper and mail. He went to the window and pulled back one of the lemon- coloured curtains. It was another foggy November morning. The skies were quite grey and a tram rattled past on its way to central London. He was hoping the skies would brighten as he was looking forward to his daily walk in Regents Park. He glanced at the headlines and sighed slightly at the state of the nation. He placed the paper on the table, sat down and began to look at the morning post. He turned over each envelope in turn. The envelope with the Edinburgh postmark was the one that caught his attention. Slightly nervous he opened the letter with the appropriate letter knife. He read the opening lines and soon a smile spread across his face. He had received good news from William Hodge and Co Ltd publishers in Scotland. The opening lines read;

Dear Sir John,

I have read with very considerable interest your account of Abraham Thornton, and I have come to the conclusion that this trial should certainly be contained in our series. If you will undertake the editing of the trial I shall be extremely obliged to you.

This was the news Sir John wanted to hear. He had been working on the Ashford case for a considerable amount of time. He had a particular interest in Trials and was especially taken by the Ashford case, because of the intriguing Appeal of Murder. After all Mr Hodge had included in the letter,

I think that the proceedings in the Appeal of Murder should be printed in full. Indeed, this is really the most important part of the case.

However, there was still an awful amount of research to be done. Sir John spent the next several weeks busily writing to those that may be able to help. Not only did Sir John enthusiastically write letters in his efforts to pursue more research on such a bizarre case; he also looked forward to every morning for the postman to come. Sir John, wearing his dressing gown, would be seated at the breakfast table. He would eventually wake up to the world after a welcomed breakfast of porridge, toast and marmalade and of course a pot of tea poured from his favourite teapot which he bought at the end of the First World War in Eastbourne.

The sound of the flap of the letterbox being opened followed by the slight thud of the morning post falling on the polished parquet floor filled Sir John with a mixture of hope and anxiety. This particular morning he received a very encouraging letter. It was typed and it was from his friend Mr Hudson, and it read as follows.

19, Cowley Street,
Westminster
S.W.1.
Telephone
Victoria 4734.

1st December 1924.

Mr dear John,

There can be little doubt that I hit upon the right person when I wrote to Birmingham about the tombstone. I send you an extract from the letter I have received (which deals also with some other questions to which I must give separate attention).

It looks to me as though it might be worthwhile for you to visit Birmingham and see Mr Powell, the Chief Librarian, and Mr W. B Bickley, who is a well known Birmingham historian, but you will decide about this when you have perused my enclosures.

Yours ever,

A Hudson.

P.S. We were both so sorry that Sophy wasn't well enough to come to us for the weekend. I hope she is really all right by this time.

Sir John Hall, Bart.

Sir John wasted no time in writing to Mr Bickley in Birmingham. On a wintry December morning soon afterwards the sound of the flap of the letterbox being opened followed by a thud on the doormat brought news from Mr Bickley.

39, Trafalgar Road,
Moseley
Birmingham

8 Dec 1924

Dear Sir,

In reply to yours of the 5th, I cannot do better than send you a list of the papers & documents I have, which are those prepared for the second trial in the Ashford case.

Sir John read on with interest.

There are 33 depositions of witnesses, some of them containing several sheets of brief, -Thornton's confession to Omar Hall, - the plan, which I consider of some value, the latter belonged to my Late Father, who actually remembered the trial, & the ballads about it being sung in the streets of Birmingham. With regard to the finale of your letter as to Thornton's innocence, I may say here that he probably had no design to take the girl's life, - far from it, - but his violence was the cause of her death.

If you would care to have a layman's opinion, I will give you mine, freely, & bluntly, & in as few words as possible. I will stay in for you on Monday next, kindly tell me if your visit will be in the morning or afternoon, oblige

Yours faithfully

Mr B. Bickley.

Sir John Hall reading relevant correspondence.

Sir John walked towards the window and stared out on the London horizon: a maze of bricked buildings lay before him. The winter sun struggled to shine through the grey clouds. Mr Bickley's letter had raised some very interesting points. Mr Bickley was obviously very knowledgeable but he must also be quite old if his father could remember the trial! But he could remember the famous ballads being sung in Birmingham. He instantly could imagine the scene. A low beamed tavern full of noise and tobacco smoke lit by oil lamps and candles, tankards of ale and men with waistcoats and collarless shirts laughing raucously and young women spurning their advances with a push of the hand and a toss of the head. A silence suddenly descends as a young woman, dressed in a pretty dress, walks to a slightly raised platform. All eyes are fixed on her and after a few moments she begins to sing.

Sir John came out of his daydream and looked at the letter again.

I may say here, that he probably had no design to take the girl's life, - far from it, - but his violence was the cause of her death.

How very intriguing, thought Sir John, how very, very intriguing this case is turning out to be. His thoughts turned once more from the fanciful to the practical. He had to make arrangements to travel to Birmingham and meet Mr Bickley; furthermore he must let Mr Bickley know at what time he was calling.

Sir John wrote immediately to him and posted the letter in the afternoon. Sir John received a letter from Mr Bickley that was written on the 10th December.

Dear Sir,

Many thanks for your letter received this morning. I will stay in for you on Monday afternoon next, about 3 o'clock.

If you do not know anything of the district, I may tell you that the easiest way to get here is by the Trafalgar Road Tram, No 41, from Navigation Street, just outside New Street Station, fare 1.1/2 – I mention this because my visitors have sometimes gone to Moseley & then had to walk back half a mile.

The last time I saw the fatal pit, (about 12 years ago I think,) it was almost dry & the sloping sides covered with bushes.

I venture to send you two notes of my own views on the Ashford Case, please do not trouble to reply we can talk the matter over on Monday.

Yours faithfully,

Mr B Bickley.

P.s. I have found another letter of Omar Hall.

Sir John smiled to himself. He afforded himself a little joke. The trail of the trial was proving to be fruitful indeed.

Chapter Twenty-one. St Winifred's Vicarage.

I can't help wonder what was discussed that Monday afternoon in Moseley. I wonder what Mr Bickley's opinions were but as they were never written down we shall never know.

It's also quite remarkable to think that Mr Bickley had visited the Fatal Field and had inspected the pit. Now, it is impossible, as houses were built on the site in the 1930's obliterating any trace of the pit.

Sir John was also interested in finding out about Mary's grave as well as the pit and Fatal Field. I came across a rather charming account written by a William Finnemore, Secretary of the Midland Liberal Federation. His letter dated November 28th 1924 was sent to Sir Robert Hudson, who, as we know, had been assisting Sir John.

As to Sir John Hall's query about the Ashford trial. As the churchyard has now ceased to be an open place except as to a carefully pallisaded walk through it, I took a lunch hour to run over myself. I knew where the grave was because, oddly enough, as a youngster when bitten by Scott's "Ivanhoe" and interested in Knights and 'gages of battle' and such like, I happened some how or other on the fact that at the trial of Abraham Thornton for the alleged murder of Mary Ashford his counsel resuscitated some forgotten statute by means of which his client was able to demand (and did) to fight the matter out with the next of kin to Mary Ashford, and threw down his 'gage of battle' in court. The position was an impossible one and he escaped, and I remember reading, (I suppose in the Reference Library) an account of the trial. Your query, therefore, was not without personal interest.

I dug out the caretakers, two very very old people, the old man decrepit with rheumatism, but the old lady put on her bonnet and shawl and came and unlocked the gate for me and we stood at the grave. The stone is the same one that was put up in 1817 but the inscription is very much worn. I found Sir John Hall's copy of the inscription was seriously faulty, and I took down the old lady's repetition of it. The verses were quite indecipherable; these she recited to me and I came away.

I know how valuable are those memories, but know how liable also they are to go astray. I therefore asked my friend, Powell, the Chief Librarian of Birmingham, to look up the matter in his local collection of books, which is a very wonderful one, and let me have a copy of the inscription, with a reference to any papers dealing with the subject. I have his letter this morning, which I send on.

As a matter of personal curiosity, I find the old lady's memory was perfectly correct. The only word I could not make out was the old lady's pronunciation of the word, "Muse" in the last line but one, which she would insist was, "maze", which

I knew could not be. Your friend will also note the contents of Powell's letter. As to the authorship of the verses I was satisfied that the initials "L.B." appeared at the bottom. The "B" was very plain, and the, "L" passably so.

Yes, it's a charming account. Again sadly, as with the pit, all that remains of Mary's grave is a slab in the ground. The first time I saw it was on a winter's afternoon during Christmas with my Birmingham friends. It had snowed quite heavily and the churchyard was a blanket of pure white. I had heard that the gravestone was near the porch of the church but that afternoon we had great difficulty in finding it. When we did it resembled nothing more than an old, moss stained paving stone, which I thought was quite sad.

The old lady was wrong and that the word is **MUSE** and not **MAZE,** although at times as the case is so baffling **MAZE** may have been more appropriate! Also, as we already know the letters **LB** are the initials of Luke Booker the Vicar of Dudley who penned the elegy to Mary. I wonder if Mr Finnemore saw any link between the old lady with her bonnet and shawl and Mary!

By the spring of 1925 according to the letters Mr Bickley wrote, Sir John had decided to concentrate on the legal side of the case. He became very interested in William Bedford, the magistrate who we know lived at Birches Green, which is now called Rookery House. It seems Mr Bedford was convinced of Thornton's guilt and pursued him like a hound does a fox. He also gave £500.0s 0d to a fund to support the Appeal and all the costs that would go with it, such as lawyers' fees, travelling expenses and so forth. This was a considerable amount of money, which would be seen as a small fortune in those days!

Mary Ashford's grave as it is today.

However, Sir John, like us, followed Thornton across the Atlantic, figuratively speaking of course. In the course of my research I came across a letter from America from an Albert Matthews to Sir John, who was then staying at Hove, near Brighton.

Albert Matthews
19, St Botolph Street
Boston
Mass.

February 21, 1925.

Dear Sir,

It is always a pleasure to respond to any request from an Englishman, and especially to one from Mr Bleakley.* I hope however, that you appreciate the difficulty of the problem you have placed before me, for on its face the outlook for any solution seems hardly likely. However, I will see what I can do with it and report to you later.

By a singular coincidence I had here, when your letter reached me, a copy of your "Bravo Mystery and Other cases," which I had just taken out of a library, and also a copy of the first volume of William O. Woodall's "Collection of Reports on Celebrated Trials," published in 1873. Though not a lawyer yet I am much interested in murder cases and have read or glanced through a great many books on the subject.

Your volume was interesting. At the end of his Thornton case, Woodhall said, "Thornton left this country after his discharge and went to New York, where he is reported to be still living." (p.74.) Of course this statement is well known to you. The data you sent me will be of great use to me, especially the name of the Shamrock and the date of its sailing, September 30th 1818. Off hand I do not know whether there are in the Boston Library any New York papers of the right date, but if there are perhaps I shall be able to run down something of value. Still as I remarked above, the chance of doing so seems slight, especially if Thornton changed his name.

Very truly yours

Albert Matthews.

Sir John Hall
Hove, England.

* I think Mr Matthews became confused with the spelling, as it should read, Mr Bickley.

Sir John did eventually publish a book entitled, "The Trial of Abraham Thornton." It can be found in the reference library in Sutton Coldfield and no doubt specialist bookshops. I have no idea what happened to Albert Matthews.

However, Sir John, Sir Robert Hudson, Mr Bickley, Mr Finnemore, and Albert Matthews are all now woven into the colourful tapestry we call history! In a way it seems as if the baton has now been passed on to keep people informed of this mystery. The mystery is once more ignited and people are attracted to the flames that burn so bright. And as they approach the fire, getting closer and closer to the heat the question remains, "Who was responsible?"

The main suspect is, of course, Thornton but there is speculation that Thornton was not the murderer, but that Mary either died by accident or suicide. In January of 1925, an aficionado of the case, Eric Watson, of 50, Bernard Street, London, wrote to Sir John and said quite plainly,

"I know the case well; only Edward Holroyd's edition is dependable – it is in effect that of his father the judge, and it alone makes it clear that the connection took place before and not after the girl had gone to Hannah Cox's to change her dancing dress and stockings. So the rape and murder charges collapsed together...."

According to Watson Thornton wasn't the murderer and therefore we must look elsewhere to find the cause of death. In order to make any sort of surmise it will be helpful I feel to present again a synopsis of the case to refresh our memory.

Midnight May 26th 1817. The dance finishes at the Tyburn and Mary, Hannah, Ben Carter and Abraham Thornton leave.

2.45. a.m. Mary and Thornton are seen talking at the bottom of the Foughdrove beside Bell Lane by John Humpage.

3.30.a.m. Mary is seen walking fast from Bell Lane towards Erdington by Thomas Asprey.

4.00. a.m. Mary is seen coming towards Erdington to Mrs Butler's house by Joseph Dawson.

4.05. a.m. Mary changes her clothes at Hannah's. Hannah talks to her as she changes.

4.15.a.m. Mary is seen coming from Hannah's carrying her bundle of clothes and going along Bell Lane in a hurry. John Kesterton saw her.

4.18.a.m. Mary is seen crossing the road from Erdington to Penn's Mill Lane by Thomas Broadhurst. This was the last time Mary is seen alive.

4.30. a.m. William Jennings, Martha Jennings, John Holden and Jane Heaton see Thornton by Holden's farm.

5.05.a.m. John Haydon, Mr Rotton's gamekeeper sees Thornton, about half a mile from Mr Holden's house. He talks with Thornton for about 15 minutes, Thornton then walks off to Castle Bromwich.

5.10.a.m. Thornton is seen passing Wheelwright's Bank by employee James

White about half a mile from Twamley's Mill.

6.00.a.m. George Jackson finds Mary in a marl pit on his way to work. Mary's bonnet, boots and bundle are found beside the pit.

Was it suicide? There is a strand of thought that suggests that after allowing Thornton to have sex with her she soon became consumed by remorse and guilt, the extent of which led her to return to the field where connection took place. Then feeling the extent of her guilt she makes her way to the brim of the pit where she places her possessions side by side on the top. After staring down into the abyss, she then throws herself into the murky water knowing that the sides being steep and slippery she would have little chance of being able to climb back up.

It is possible that Mary did take her own life but it raises certain questions. She appeared calm and in good spirits when she returned to Hannah's. She was not distressed or agitated in any way. (Unless of course Hannah lied!). Furthermore, if she did commit suicide how can the bruises be accounted for on her arms and even more significantly who was the owner of the male footprints found at the top of the marl pit? Also the newspaper of the day, Aris's Birmingham Gazette reported on Monday 2nd June that Mary as,

"Having many marks of violence on her, particularly about the head."

Although this contradicts the evidence of the coroner's court, it is obvious violence took place, violent marks that would not have been endured by throwing oneself into a pit of water.

Another theory is that Mary died by accident. She had willingly gone into a field with Thornton, thought nothing more of it and went back to Hannah's to change. On her way back to her uncle's Mr Coleman, she noticed just how much blood had leaked onto her clothing and went to the pit to clean herself. However, she fell in and was unable to get out. She did not have the strength to clamber out as she was now exhausted from the walking and dancing.

However, if this is the case, again, the marks on her arms cannot be explained away nor the footprints. Also, why would she go to a disused marl pit to clean herself when a small river, the Plantsbrook, is in full flow, only a matter of yards away?

If it is not suicide, if it is not an accident then it has to be **MURDER.**

THE CASE FOR.

Thornton was the last person to be seen in her company before she died.

He had a reputation as a ladies' man and was reputed to have said about Mary, "I will connect with her or die!"

He lied about walking Mary back to Hannah Cox's as she was seen alone by **TWO** independent witnesses, Asprey and Dawson.

He said he waited for her on the village green in Erdington. Yet Kesterton the waggoner, who saw Mary come out of the entry of Hannah's said no one else was on the road and that the road was clear and he could see for quite a distance.

Thornton's footprints were discovered near the scene of the crime.

He admitted having sex with her and there was blood on his shirt.

He admitted raping her and throwing her into the pit to Omar Hall whilst in custody.

He had a letter confessing his guilt stolen by a Liverpool prostitute.

The contents of the box at Black Hawk Hall were tantamount to a confession.

THE CASE AGAINST.

He had an alibi.

Shortly after Mary's death he was seen over two miles away at Castle Bromwich.

Not only was he seen, he was seen first by **FOUR** witnesses by Holden's farm and then another **FOUR** shortly afterwards. All swore in a court of law that they had seen him at the time of Mary's death or thereabouts.

He openly admitted having sex with Mary and never tried to hide the fact, which in turn showed his honesty.

Mary lied. She told Hannah that she had stayed at her Grandfather's when in reality she was in a field copulating with Thornton. She was too embarrassed or ashamed to tell Hannah.

One of the footprints in the harrowed field were of a boot with a nail missing and although his boot had a nail missing it did not prove that it was his boot as there could be lots of boots with nails missing!

Omar Hall fabricated the whole story in order to get himself a pardon.

The tale of the letter and the Liverpool prostitute is pure myth.

There never was any "Black box."

Before the second trial he could have easily left the country and gone to America. Instead, he decided to stay and clear his name.

Before a decision is made it is helpful to remind ourselves of further facts.

As we have discovered, Erdington and Castle Bromwich worked on two different time zones suggesting that the evidence of the clocks could be unreliable. Also, we know that if the clocks were tampered with before the court officials checked them, then the evidence is made redundant. It is also possible that if there was any collusion with Thornton the clocks could have been altered **AFTER** the murder and therefore giving Thornton an alibi.

Constable Dale's disposition was discredited and was discharged from the police force soon after the first trial. His evidence was quite crucial in securing a, "Not guilty" verdict for Thornton. Rumour had it that the jurors were not twelve good men honest and free!

Also a focal point of evidence lies with the clothing of the deceased. Remember Mary changed back into her working clothes. That is she changed her dress and stockings but for some reason did not change her shoes. She kept her dancing shoes on and carried her working shoes. This is extremely significant.

Mary's body was found with her spencer ripped and there was a lot of blood around the genitals, which indicated intercourse by force, and furthermore there were splashes of blood on her dancing shoes. When Mary changed, Hannah was in the room. Hannah, according to her testimony, did not see any blood either on Mary's body or clothes. She certainly didn't see any blood on her shoes neither did she see a ripped spencer. It can be argued that she changed in dim light and therefore there was not sufficient light for Hannah to see. However, Hannah and Mary were best friends surely if Mary was in distress either physically or emotionally she would have confided in Hannah.

Now, if Hannah hadn't noticed any blood on her shoes whilst at her house it seems as if the **CONNECTION** took place **AFTER** Mary left Hannah's. The argument against this is that when Mary's body was taken from the pit there wasn't any blood on her stockings. This suggests that connection took place **BEFORE** she returned to Hannah's.

However, Mary's working stockings were made of dark wool and any blood would have been absorbed into the fabric when placed in water. (I know this because I consulted a wardrobe mistress at a leading professional theatre.)

It may have helped to solve the case if Mary had changed her shoes. If she had changed into her working shoes and the dancing shoes were not bloodstained then it suggests that Mary did not start bleeding either by menstruation or violent assault until **AFTER** leaving Hannah's. Also if she had changed her footwear the female footprints in the harrowed field would have been easily determined. If the prints in the field were her dancing shoes then Thornton's version is true. If however, she had worn her working shoes on the way back to Langley Heath then it must have been Thornton who chased her that night. A simple act of not changing shoes has helped the case remain a mystery for all this time!

I think we can safely say that it certainly was not suicide or an accident. However, if Thornton is innocent then what is perhaps more intriguing is quite simply, "Who did it?" The eyes of suspicion then fall on Benjamin Carter, boyfriend of Hannah.

Let's remember he went back to the Tyburn House to retrieve a bracelet for Hannah. Was this a stalling tactic to allow Hannah and he to be separated? We also don't know of Carter's movements any time after midnight. Could he have followed Mary and Thornton and become enraged with jealousy as he watched the lovers under the May moonlight? It may seem far-fetched but it should not be discounted with a mere wave of the hand.

However, if it wasn't Thornton and it wasn't Carter who was it? One strain of a theory is that it was Thomas Broadhurst who was the last person to see Mary alive as she walked home to Sutton. I suppose it is possible that he was suddenly over taken by lust of demonic proportions and chased after Mary and committed the crime. However, the footprints found at the scene clearly show that Mary was confronted by some one who stood in her way and was facing her whilst Broadhurst would have come from the opposite direction. It seems therefore, Broadhurst is vindicated, who after a night of indulgence was innocently making his way home to bed!

As we must examine all possibilities it is possible that a stranger with psychopathic tendencies happened to be wandering around at that time in the morning and seeing a young woman on her own attacked and killed her.

The last of the theories is that Thornton did kill her but not until he established an alibi for himself. He then went back to the fatal field where he met Mary around 6.00 and murdered her. Out of all the theories this along with the wandering psychopath is probably the weakest as George Jackson discovered Mary's body around 6.00 and the question has to be asked why would Mary be waiting for him?

It is probably the statement of Bickley, the Moseley historian that seems to be the most pertinent,

I may say here, that he probably had no design to take the girl's life, - far from it, - but his violence was the cause of her death.

This can be interpreted in various ways. After forcing himself on her and finding himself in danger of being arrested, he flung the girl into the pit, or that the rape of Mary led her to commit suicide, an option that has more or less been discounted.

History has ordained it that the mystery of Mary Ashford would not become just a tale told around a fireside at winter. Not only has the case featured in many legal papers and debates over the years but also Mary has become a "cause celebre" in feminist politics and thinking. Anna Clarke writing for the New Society magazine, (August 1986) wrote a very thought-provoking article entitled, "Rewriting the history of rape." In the article Anna Clarke argues that community outrage is not enough and that the problem of male violence and its prevention needs deeper analysis and attention. The article prints one of the popular songs of Mary's day, which acted as a warning to young women.

Now all you virgins that bloom as I bloom'd
Keep at home in your proper employ;
Ne'ere in dancing delight,
Nor in the fields roam, With a stranger from home,
Lest you meet a fate as wretched as I.

It is dreadfully unfair that women are penalized, made fearful, are not allowed to enjoy the pleasures of the world such as dancing and walking in the countryside because of the threat of male violence. Instead of addressing the issue of male violence middle class reforms led to working class women like Mary to being restrained in their social and personal life. Therefore, it was working class women who had to control and change their lives and not the perpetrators of the law!

Anna Clarke also makes a very important point when she says,

"Contemporary melodramas performed in London and Birmingham portrayed Thornton as an aristocrat who bribed the jury to acquit him although he was a bricklayer."

Thornton's lawyers and those opposed to him endeavoured to demonize him, make him look mad and bad almost a Frankenstein figure. However, the truth is much more disturbing. Thornton was an ordinary man, who farmed the land, drank and danced like most of his contemporaries. He wasn't a vicious beast lurking in a dark alley as usually depicted in Hollywood movies. He was a young man with free will who had the capacity to do good or evil, like all of us. If guilty then yes, he committed the most pernicious and evil act a human being can commit. He was no demon but carried out the work of the devil. As Clarke says,

"Was, in fact, Mary Ashford's death a 'date rape' with fatal consequences.?"

Likewise a film entitled "Property Rights" looked at the case from a feminist historical perspective and a similar theme to Anna Clarke's in that male violence is carried out not by vicious beasts but ordinary male members of the community. It was a successful film and was screened on Channel Four television. The film along with many academic articles published on the case fundamentally looks at, not only male violence towards women but as with the New Society article, looks at the attitude and consequent action that follows it. For example, the Reverend Luke Booker who wrote the inscription on Mary's gravestone stated that Mary had gone, "To a place of amusement without proper recourse of protection." There is a subtext here, which clearly states that Mary was in some way at fault! Furthermore it insinuates that women have to be protected from men by men! Although the case is shrouded in mystery it clearly conveys facts that can be brought in the arena for debate where feminist philosophy plays a role and history can be seen through the eyes of women. One could argue that despite a heinous crime having been committed Mary's death has acted, in some way, as a catalyst for female emancipation, which can only be seen as good.

However, the reality of murder, its brutality, its violence, its pointless waste of life was to rear its ugly head once more in Erdington and it would be too disturbing to belong to the realm of fireside storytelling.

For now the story may be told in form of a synopsis. On the 28th May 1989 the Mail on Sunday published a fascinating article entitled,

TALE OF A HAUNTING MURDER MYSTERY.

The article was written by Chester Stern and it read,

"Bizarre coincidences between two unsolved murder cases have been uncovered by the Crown Prosecution Service researchers.

An anonymous note sent to the Director of Public Prosecutions late last year urged investigators to probe similarities between the two crimes.

This week the CPS records officer reported to the DPP:

"On Whit Monday, May 26 1817, a young woman, who lived in the West Midlands travelled to Birmingham. She changed her dress at a friend's house and went on to a dance. In the early hours of Whit Monday she was sexually assaulted and murdered near the Chester Road in the Pype Hayes area.

A man named Thornton was arrested and charged. At the trial he was acquitted. 157 years later in 1974 Whit Sunday again fell on a May 26. A young woman travelled from her home north of Birmingham. She changed her dress at a friend's house and went to a dance. In the early hours she got off a bus in Chester Road near Pype Hayes. Her body was later found near the road. She had also been sexually assaulted. A man was later acquitted of murdering her. His name – Thornton."

So, after a hundred and fifty seven years, another tragedy took place in Erdington. Although there are some inaccuracies in the article it is quite astonishing. (I.e. Mary went to the dance on Whit Monday not on Whit Sunday.) Furthermore, who sent the anonymous note to the Director of Public prosecutions? It is also

The old rambling Jacobean Pype Hayes Hall and grounds. What secrets does it hold?

62

interesting to remember that the CPS took the matter seriously.

It has also come to light that the young woman in 1974 was, like Mary, at the time of her death, twenty years of age. Then there are the similarities; both young women were returning from, "A place of amusement." Both had worn new dresses especially for the occasion. The day they were murdered was May 27th. Those responsible were never brought to justice. Two men accused of the crime and later acquitted were both, as we have discovered, called Thornton!

In 1974 the young woman who died, Barbara Forrest, worked at Pype Hayes Hall, a rambling, mysterious Jacobean house, which Mary would have known. In fact whoever attacked Mary his footsteps were found running by the side of the hall. There is a story that on the night Barbara was killed two colleagues working in the hall experienced a storm around the old house. However, it was later proved not even a drop of rain had fallen that night. In 1816 the year before Mary died an earthquake took place in Erdington!

If the Mary Ashford case was not steeped in mystery enough it seems there is a series of bizarre co-incidences that attached to the case that take place 157 years to the day. Is it solely co-incidence, the laws of probability at work? Or is it something stranger, more unfathomable?

As to what really happened that May night in 1817, I leave it to you, my dear friend and reader to decide.

Father Martin
St Winifred's Vicarage.
Lower Stretton
Worcestershire.

March 2002.

APPENDIX - Scene of the crime

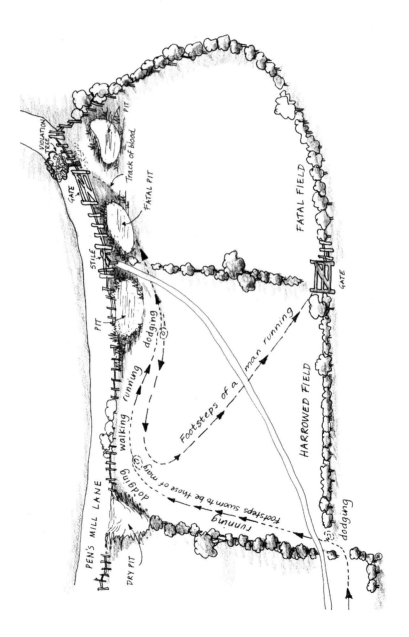

Postscript by the author.

As you will have read, the case of Mary Ashford is indeed a tragic one and you now know how Mary, a young woman of twenty lost her life. The death of any young person evokes both anger and grief. However, that anger and grief is compounded if the death could have been avoided. Everyone born into this world has the right to life and no human being has the right to take that life away.

Due to the nature of the case the Mary Ashford Society has decided to donate the Royalties of the book to charity.

The charities that will benefit from the sale of One Morning in May are as follows:

Birmingham Women's Aid.

Birmingham Women's Aid believes that women have the right to live from violence, abuse and fear. The charity provides support services and safe refuge accommodation for women and children affected by domestic violence, rape and sexual abuse. The organization also works with young people in schools to raise awareness of domestic violence and to explore ways of building healthy positive relationships.

For further information please telephone the Helpline on 0121 685 8550.

Rape and Sexual Violence Project.

The Rape and Sexual Violence Project is a charity offering a telephone helpline and counselling service to survivors of rape, sexual assault and childhood sexual abuse. The project supports females and male survivors, their families, friends and partners.

For further information please telephone the Helpline on 0121 233 3818.

Dr Barnado.

Dr Barnado's supports work with abused, disadvantaged and excluded children and young people, including those exploited and abused through prostitution

Themis.

The Mary Ashford Society will also be assisting, *Themis* a charity in Madrid, which supports victims of domestic violence.

On behalf of the Mary Ashford Society I want to thank you for supporting the vital and crucial work the above charities provide.

All best wishes,

Patrick B Hayes. - Secretary, Mary Ashford Society.

BY THE SAME AUTHOR:

Ghost Stories of Erdington
Ghost Stories of Sutton Coldfield
We'll Meet Again